adultery and c

Farrukh Dhondy was born in Pune in 1944. After graduating in physics from Wadia College, he won a scholarship to Cambridge to train as a quantum physicist but ended up reading for a BA in English. He has lived in England since and has worked as a teacher, and as a commissioning editor at Channel 4 television. Dhondy's first collection of stories, *East End at Your Feet*, was published in 1977. He is the author of *Come to Mecca*, *Run!*, *Poona Company*, *Bombay Duck*, and *C.L.R. James: A Life*. He also writes screenplays for films, television, and for the stage.

adultery and other stories

Farrukh Dhondy

HarperCollins *Publishers* India
a joint venture with

New Delhi

First published in India in 2011 by
HarperCollins *Publishers* India
a joint venture with
The India Today Group

Copyright © Farrukh Dhondy 2011

ISBN: 978-93-5029-107-8

2 4 6 8 10 9 7 5 3 1

Farrukh Dhondy asserts the moral right
to be identified as the author of this work.

This is a work of fiction and all characters and incidents described in this book are
the product of the author's imagination. Any resemblance to actual persons, living or
dead, is entirely coincidental.

HarperCollins *Publishers*
A-53, Sector 57, Noida 201301, India
77-85 Fulham Palace Road, London W6 8JB, United Kingdom
Hazelton Lanes, 55 Avenue Road, Suite 2900, Toronto, Ontario M5R 3L2
and 1995 Markham Road, Scarborough, Ontario M1B 5M8, Canada
25 Ryde Road, Pymble, Sydney, NSW 2073, Australia
31 View Road, Glenfield, Auckland 10, New Zealand
10 East 53rd Street, New York NY 10022, USA

Typeset in Ehrhardt MT Std 11/15

Printed and bound at
Thomson Press (India) Ltd.

To TD, SD, JD, DD, TSD and LP

contents

ONE

boogoo

Yes, she was bored with me and I shouldn't say I was bored with her, because I felt towards her as a snake must towards a snake-charmer. I was strangely dependent on her and she materially on me; and I danced to her tunes, familiar tunes. And there the metaphor is reversed, because it was not I but she who disappeared into the thickets now and then only to return to the comforts of the basket in a while.

We had furious arguments. She left her computer on once and I, shamelessly, leafed through her messages and found that she had joined an Internet dating agency and was corresponding with some man in France who said his wife had died and he loved classical music, pop and folk and was especially wedded to philosophical pursuits. Later, in another e-mail, after they had exchanged distant endearments, he said he was now convinced that he had seen her aura coming off screen, that the energy that flowed through her words would revitalize the spirit that had died in him after the devastating demise of his wife who was, like Elvis, still alive, etc.

The poor fellow characterized his own misguided ramblings as 'philosophy'. I thought of Aristotle, Aquinas, Kant and

Hegel turning in their graves. It was curious. It only increased my contempt for Teresa's mind, which I once took, oh ages ago, to be keen, untutored, but willing to learn.

The French fool kept quoting Kahlil Gibran in his mails. It was one of his techniques of seduction and it, to my disappointment, seemed to have succeeded.

At the same time, Teresa was working – or 'turning' as they say in the old profession – other tricks on the Internet. There were messages to and from some British half-wit with a boat – his prized possession – on the Riviera on which he was offering Trea, Teresa, my partner of several precious years, a ride.

I had no right, but I scrolled through and found her pathetic replies. She said she was single and that she too loved classical music. Her hobbies were reading and keeping fit, and that her constant study was nature. Trea wouldn't know Mozart from mozzarella and her acquaintance with nature extended to mowing grass. The Internet is the liars' paradise but the shamelessness of the capture-a-partner-with-a-pack-of-lies brigade is a modern study in mental deviance.

Poor Trea, what had I done to her for her to seek solace in the arms of some idiot whose purpose in life was going for boat rides and killing foxes who had never done him any harm? The British have always struck me as being strange that way. Their imperial day is long gone but they – a defeated class who inherit their furniture and china – persist in torturing and killing horses, foxes, badgers, pheasants, dogs and anything else that can't fight back. They try and maintain the imperial accent which appeals to females of the class with dreams of gentility, but are for the most part clumsy, impotent or harbouring some deep-seated, even defeated perversion.

Such were the people my lovely, alluring, once-loved Trea was contacting and speaking to in those mounting and sad clichés on her e-mails or when I was on TV assignments around the world. She would park our only dear and perceptive child with a rota of friends or with the child's grandparents and venture into sexual adventure with the French loser and then with one or another unsatisfactory British inadequate – inadequate for her and for the harsher world outside their country lairs.

What she did on these journeys is another, and possibly her own, story but she returned from them chastened and confessional. She was born an Irish Catholic, after all.

We would discuss these excursions only when I caught her in some lie and our manner of discussion would be my conniving admission that she had been forced to stray through my neglect, bad habits, Indian assumptions and meanness. She sincerely believed that what she did was my fault, attributable in the end to me and so it was I who should be given a second, third or umpteenth chance. There would be no sign of repentance from her. I would have to stay and pretend nothing had taken place. The family motto would flash through my mind: 'The Intelligent Must Make Concessions'. Was it inertia or the hope that something would give – that Trea would change?

Of course I didn't want to lose her. She was one of my weaknesses and weaknesses become part of one. Did Achilles cut off his heel? Othello would have done otherwise, but the fact was that I was no longer attracted to Trea in any way. It was over in the sensual sense. The sight and smell of her, the only factors that drew me to her in those early years, had long since turned from the elegance of Jekyll to the grotesqueness of Hyde.

I now noticed every blackening of the veins under her eyes, each sag of skin under her chin and the developing birds' feet at the edge of her brows.

Nothing she had experienced would have induced her to re-evaluate her stance towards me or our child, towards other people or the world. In the end, I had concluded that her sense of self depended on never admitting to needing or making a reassessment. I was wrong.

In some self-punishing way, I had set myself this test of stamina. I had stuck with her and carried her emotionally and financially this decade and a half and it made me feel a better man than all the Gunga Dins she had picked up and exhausted in a matter of weeks, months, sometimes just days.

It was an unusual encounter that proved me wrong and made me reassess Trea's ability, in deep middle age, to reassess and reorient herself.

She had left one day with her suitcase, leaving a note saying this time she was really in love and was going for ever – a note which only made me smirk before I returned to my computer. I left it where I found it so she could read it when she returned – which she did. I didn't question her about where she'd been or indeed why she'd returned. I suggested instead that she come with me to India. I had work to do there. My TV crews were going to film a series. We would fly to Bombay and travel down to Poona on the *Deccan Queen* as we had done once before in the early days of our relationship.

I didn't think she would accept but she immediately agreed. She had returned from her latest adventure somewhat tamed but I never found out why. Our conversation about it followed the same pattern. She complained that she had branched out because I never took her anywhere. I was, of course, to blame. In fact, this was obvious to her twisted mind, just as suggesting that we travel to India together was to her tantamount to my admitting my guilt. She accepted it as a sign of my repentance. Self-consciousness was not her strongest quality.

We slept together that night after she wiped out a bottle of wine, took me by the wrist and wordlessly lead me to her bed where she undressed. I noticed that she had deep bruises on her thighs and on her side. I didn't ask how she had come by them. She could have fallen in the boat or been gored by a bull in Pamplona.

I was not even curious. We were to set out for London the next day and then planned to go to India. Part of my work in India was tracking down Rajesh, a young man I used to know in my teens in Bombay. We called him Raggy. It was after I left India, after we all graduated from college and I went to England, that I heard he had become one of the most successful art photographers in the country. I had known him as a skilful painter. He exhibited other skills even then. His expertise was in emptying cigarettes of tobacco and packing them with cannabis, leaving them looking like the original factory-packed cylinders; in finding bootleg liquor in the back alleys of the town and serially seducing girls with his long hair, unsettled looks and pre-hippy hippy ways.

He came from a rich family but had been disowned by them because he denounced their capitalistic wealth, profligacy and superstitions. I knew that he broke with his family when he went to art school somewhere else in the country. His father bribed the art school in Bombay to bar his entry.

He emerged years later as a self-made photographer–artist. Friends sent me clippings from the newspapers about him and copies of the photographic and illustrated books he had published.

Then there were peculiar stories about Raggy being arrested, tried and sent to jail, and about his quarrels with a publisher and about him having assaulted a very influential newspaper proprietor. He had always, in his boyhood, been good natured and gave off an air of complete laid-back calm. Though yes, he had fought with his family and always had something nasty to say about his father, his teachers, the sadhus and pretenders his mother patronized and anyone who had power over him. Now perhaps these figures had been replaced by his employers, editors, publishers or patrons – if indeed, artistic photographers have patrons.

Trea had said, as we made love, that she would 'adore' to come with me. It would be a second honeymoon. She recalled how we had first travelled from Bombay to Poona on the *Deccan Queen*, sitting wedged in the open door of the train as it climbed the ghats from the coastal strip to the Deccan Plateau.

It had been the season of drizzle and clouds on this low mountain pass. It was her first visit to India and as we sat in the railway compartment doorway facing the valleys and forested slopes, she had pointed out the troops of monkeys crossing the winding road. I told her that as children we would count the twenty-eight tunnels the train went through and she began the count, but lost it in other, more interesting adult observations.

Her reminiscences interrupted our rare sexual encounter. She was perfectly capable of crying out with what seemed startled pleasure one moment and lapsing into some thought or conversation the next.

I lay back and listened.

Yes, it would be good, I said.

I had an address for Raggy in Poona, now called Pune. I had other people to look up and things to do, but on our first morning I hustled Trea out of the hotel and into a rickshaw and gave the driver the address. The rickshaw took us into the old part of town through narrow, grumbling streets and we finally stopped outside a new office building. We got out. The street number of the building matched the address I had been given. However, the new but small building, squeezed between two ancient nineteenth-century dwellings in need of demolition themselves, housed the office of an insurance company. There was a security guard in khaki loitering at the door to keep out the riff-raff who inhabited the streets of this part of town.

'You've got the wrong place. You always think you know where you're going, but this is obviously not where your famous photographer lives. You dragged me out without breakfast. I want a cappuccino ...'

I went up the marble steps of the new building and asked the security man if there was a flat above the insurance company's offices. The first and second floor were also part of the office, he replied.

I turned to see that Trea, throwing her Brit-woman's fit in a crowded Indian street, had gathered a small cluster of

onlookers around her. I went down the steps. She was asking
these people whether there was a Starbucks anywhere nearby
and they didn't seem to know what she meant.

'Looks like this *is* the wrong address,' I said.

'You are looking for some address?' one of the idlers who
had been drawn to stare at Trea asked.

'I've found the address. I am looking for a photographer
called Rajesh. I was told he lived here.'

Two of the idlers looked at each other.

'Yes, one photograph man was here, but he sold house and
gone and this new peoples come.'

'Do you know where he went?'

The idler shook his head.

'No ideas.'

'Would any of the neighbours know?'

'We are good neighbours,' the man said and looked at the
other fellow as though they were in a conspiracy of silence.
The other man abandoned the conspiracy

'He has gone in jail,' he said.

'I am dying for a cappuccino,' Trea said.

We stopped an auto-rickshaw and I asked the diver to go
back to the hotel. Trea leaned over to the driver and asked
him to find us a coffee shop. She must have made herself
understood above the unsilenced fart of the auto-rickshaw
because the driver drove us to a modern mall which advertised
a smart coffee shop, an Indian version of Starbucks. She was
resentful, but determined. Nothing but stubborn, and in
pursuit of self-satisfaction, my Trea.

An old friend, a member of the college gang of which

Raggy and I were a part, told me the story. Raggy was jailed, not for the assault on the newspaper magnate, but for fraud. He spent a few years inside and then his father, who was still not reconciled to his ways, bribed an appeal court judge and Raggy was released. He refused help and rehabilitation from his father and moved out of town. Rumour had it that he had built his own house in some inaccessible part of the country and now lived there with his girlfriend whose mobile phone was the only link they had to the outside world. And did the friend have this phone number? No, but he thought that the instructors at the Yogic Shastra Alternative Health Institute, where she used to work, would have it.

That's where we went and a young lady gave us the phone number.

'Do you have any creams to get rid of facial wrinkles?' Trea asked.

'Of course we are selling creams, but we are recommending that patients learn ancient Indian dance techniques for the face muscles to keep everything young. You can join classes,' the young lady said, 'and regulate diet.'

'Makes sense. Is cappuccino allowed?' I asked.

'No stimulaytants,' the young lady said.

'Ah, not for our Trea, then,' I said.

We had the phone number. A deep, gentle voice answered the phone. I said I was a friend of Rajesh's and asked if I could speak to him. A process of screening? I gave her my name.

'Hey dude! I can't believe this! Where the fuck are you? How the fuck did you get hold of this number, man? God! I think about you all the time. You are a famous TV-wallah! Are you calling from London?'

'No, I'm in town. Poona.'

'Incredible! Deadly! You're coming here, aren't you? You sound the same. There's no one I want to see more.'

'Where's *here*? Tell me. You are the main reason I'm in Poona and I've had some hassle tracking you, man.'

We were back to the cadences of the college talk of our generation.

'Me? Why *me*? I've let the world go by in my pursuit of oblivion.'

'Shut up, yaar! I want to look through your photos and paintings of Raj buildings and things.'

'Doing a programme? I've given up all that shit.'

'But you've got the photographs. I heard you had the only archive of monuments and statues that have been destroyed.'

'Fuck man, I travelled seven years to get that stuff together and these arseholes cheated me, man. There's no place for honesty in this world, baby. It's dog eat dog and they bite before they bark. Hah!' That was rehearsed.

'But hey, have you got the photographs?'

'So, you're not interested in your old amigo, just the photographs, eh? Old Parsi vulture! Just kidding, man. Yeah, of course I have them. Thousands. When are you coming?'

'How do I get there?'

'No way except drive in a tough car,' he said.

'To where? How long?'

'Relax. Get a big sheet of paper and a pencil and I'll dictate a map,' he said.

He did and he was good at it. The directions were elaborate but precise. It was two hundred miles into the interior and well off the beaten track. In fact, there were times when there was hardly any track at all. The nearest village was twenty miles from the lake on which Raggy had built his wood-and-brick house.

The house was in a forested area of the vast plateau that forms the lower triangle of the Indian subcontinent. We had traversed dust roads in a hired car with a driver who had, despite the precise directions Raggy had dictated, to get out and ask villagers where the next indicated landmark was. We crossed wooded hills, meandered through winding and barren rocky volcanic passes, and then saw this valley below with a village on its fringe with the forestry track leading up and round. We could see the waters of the lake, strangely brown, and we began our descent towards it. The road in front of us disappeared into the vegetation again, the trees thick with birds, a herd of deer crossing our path; and then as we hit bottom, we finally sighted the clearing and the house.

Raggy had heard the engine of the car and was waiting for us. It had taken us five hours more than his calculations and Trea had started to moan and complain. She was convinced that my map was wrong, that the river should have been on our right and not our left, that we would end up lost and spending the night in the car, and she was resentful and scratchy.

But we got there.

As we got out of the car and Raggy came up and hugged me, I could see he was actually looking at Trea, a masculine assessment. Then he gave her a hug.

'Mi casa, su casa. I built it with my own hands. Villagers and the spirits of the forest helped me,' he said.

As he led us to the entrance, the young woman whose phone we had used, the lifeline to this haven, emerged from the house.

Raggy introduced her proudly.

'Vinnayana,' he said.

She folded her hands in greeting.

'She doesn't like to be called Vinny,' he added.

'You *can* call me Vinny,' she said, stealing an admonitory glance at Raggy.

'I'm called Trea,' Teresa said.

'A good vibe, a good omen,' Vinnayana said.

'And your name! Not one heard before. Very pretty,' I said.

'It means "conscious thought",' Raggy said.

We went into the house. The front door led straight into an open-plan room which had only three walls. Where the fourth wall should have been was blue sky, the opening to the lake whose waters were just a few feet away from the foundations. From this room a twenty-foot jetty protruded on wooden stilts into the waters.

It would have been breathtaking had my breath not already been stolen by the sight and grace of Vinnayana. She was stunning. A dark, slender beauty with paisley eyes and the alluring, deep, measured voice that had first cast its spell through the phone. I was staring at her and Trea caught me looking.

Vinnayana was asking if we would like a drink.

'No alcohol and no stimulants, I'm afraid,' she said and there was in the apology a challenge. We had come to her Nirvana and we were being initiated into its rules.

'Man, I suffer,' Raggy said.

'Fruit juice or goat's milk, or lassi. Plenty of choice,' Vinnayana said.

'Look, I know him, he doesn't travel without a bottle of whisky in his back pocket. You can bring it out, no objection,' Raggy said. It was a little act of defiance.

'Those days are long past,' I said. 'No whisky, but I did bring you a couple of bottles of Indian white wine. Sula's Sauvignon Blanc. I didn't know booze was taboo. Sorry!'

'Hey, bring it in, man, what are we talking about? Because Vinny doesn't drink, *we* all don't have to become Mahatma Gandhi!'

I looked at Vinnayana. She smiled a beautiful smile. She was wearing a sarong and a tight Rajasthani blouse with mirror-work which showed off her near-spherical brown breasts which seemed just a trifle overblown for her lean frame. Beside her, Trea with her scattered pink complexion, broad back and large bones, wearing jeans and a man's shirt to hide the fat on her waist, looked clumsy, unprepossessing. For the first time I wondered if somewhere in my subconscious I had dragged Trea with me in order to make this comparison with the Indian women of my memory and so force an aesthetic decision on myself. I must, somewhere in the recesses of the dormant possessiveness and jealousy, have been resentful of her serial adultery and have a yearning to ditch her or, as she would see it, set her free.

But there were things at stake. The child would remain in boarding school and we would do what endless numbers of emotionally incompetent British divorced couples do: 'sharing the responsibility', dividing the time according to some court judgement, devising trips to the cinema and seaside and dragging the reluctant child along on holidays till the poor girl went her own neglected, dysfunctional way.

Vinnayana flashed her perfect white teeth in a dimpled smile.

'No taboos. Nothing is forbidden. All discipline has to be self-discipline. It comes from inside.'

'So go and fetch the wine, baby,' Raggy said. 'Haven't had a drink in six months and you are my excuse and she really doesn't mind. The road of excess leads to the palace of wisdom.'

I went to the car to fetch the wine. The driver was asleep, stretched across the back seat. I fetched our bags. *It comes from inside!* Those were really the first words she had uttered and there was a falseness to them, a *pretence* that this was a deep and realized wisdom; the fact was the words and the pious tone were those of homilies mugged up from some self-improvement charlatan's book.

I gave the bottles to Raggy who fetched some strings, tied them to the necks of the bottles which he lowered into the lake, tying the ends of the strings to the jetty's post. He fetched two chairs, apparently ones he had fashioned himself, to the jetty.

'No fridge,' he said, 'we are saving the planet. All the electricity we use comes from solar plates on the roof.'

'Does it work?'

'No,' he said, 'but it makes us feel virtuous. We have to collect a lot of firewood for cooking and light candles when the batteries run flat, which they do every hour.' There was no edge of irony in his voice. These were matters of fact.

Vinnayana was showing Trea around the house.

'It's delightful' was Trea's verdict when she emerged, dodging the low wooden lintel of the bedroom door. I looked at the ceiling of the open front room. It was made of logs milled flat by some local machinery because the planks weren't properly rectangular and had wavy edges through which one could see the corrugated iron roof.

Raggy proudly explained how he had tackled the construction. He had to figure out the engineering himself and some men from the local mill, who brought the shipment of village-made rough bricks on bullock carts, had stayed for months, living in improvised jungle huts, to help him dig and fill the foundations. The solar panels came from the city and the only oil-burning luxury they allowed themselves was a little outboard motor which they had fixed to the boat which came with the lakeside land they had bought. It didn't seem to bother them that burning wood also produced carbon dioxide.

I said I'd like a tour of the house too. I wanted to see the shape this dream had taken.

'I had to, I had to,' he said about the construction. 'It was not ambition or a matter of choice. I went to jail, you know, and for the first time in my life I took the cash that grandfather had left me and bought this place. I hate India, man,' he said. It was the last thing I had expected him to say.

'There are jobs for photographers abroad,' I said.

He showed me the room they used as a dining room and the outhouse kitchen with the moulded earthen stove. There were no doors inside the house but each doorway was draped with a thick curtain. A door draped with a blue curtain led off the dining room, leading to the last room of the house. As we returned from the outhouse kitchen, Raggy put his fingers to his lips and whispered, 'Let's see what Harry is doing.' He could have been talking about a pet turtle.

He pushed the curtain aside and seemed to invite me to enter the room, which I did. It was the second largest room in the house with a wooden trestle bed: waist high, narrow and with a thin mattress on it. Bizarrely, this bed stood in the centre of the room as an operating table would. The rest of the room was sparse with a cupboard and two fancy leather suitcases next to it. There was a tank fixed to the ceiling which caught and filtered rain water and drained into the basin, which stood in the room, through a rubber pipe. On the bed, a white man in a white kurta squatted cross-legged in the pose of the Buddha, his eyes lightly shut. He may have heard our footsteps and the rustle of the curtain, but he gave no sign of it.

Raggy looked at his watch. Then he spoke aloud as though the man were not in the room at all.

'Harry is Vinny's patient. He came to us from the USA and moved in to be under her guidance 24/7.'

Harry didn't open his eyes or change his meditative serious expression of counterfeit tranquillity.

'Patient?' I was whispering.

'Yeah,' Raggy said without any effort at keeping his voice down. 'Harry has what the doctors call rampant and terminal cancer. He'd be dead by now, but Vinny has taken him on, and is curing him with her skills. The cancer is already on the run and going. A slow sunrise.'

'Cure cancer?'

'Man, it had spread all over: pancreas, spleen. Like, the US doctors even at the best clinic in NY said he was a goner. Ask the man himself when he comes out of meditation.'

'Ask me now,' said Harry in a high-pitched voice, pronouncing 'ask' as 'eyusk'.

He hopped off the bed to demonstrate his vigour, not very convincingly since he had to stretch his hand back to the mattress to steady himself.

'She is a Goddess,' he said. 'My Goddess. The rot has been stemmed. See, cancer doesn't come from the outside; it's the will to life that's been tampered with. It's not a live virus; it's like a computer virus in the patterns of energy. Life is spirit. The computer is the balance of energies of the spirit and that's what you gotta get in check.'

It was a speech he knew by heart and was dying to repeat.

'You got all that?' He grinned.

There couldn't have been many listeners whom he could tell, or joke with about the telling. Perhaps Vinnayana and he repeated variations of the speech to each other every now and then.

'She's bringing everything she knows to it, man. And that's sorting it out. According to his sons, Harry should have been pushing up the daisies and those daisies should have been two feet high by now.'

'Daisies don't grow two feet,' Harry said. He sounded as he must have in days gone by, when he was a short, stocky, tight-skinned American businessman rather than a professional patient and the soul-spirit-and-DNA-cell tamer.

He stretched his hand out to indicate that he would follow us out of the meditation room which was also, the suitcases indicated, his living quarters.

We went back to the living room and found Trea and Vinnayana sitting on the jetty where our wine was cooling under the diffuse orange and pink of the setting sun. Harry followed us and, as he approached Vinnayana, folded his arms in front of him and bowed for ten seconds in a parody of a Japanese ritual greeting. Vinnayana took no notice. She smiled but continued talking to Trea. She must have told Trea about Harry because Trea looked at him without the least surprise.

We opened the screw-topped wine bottle and drank wine from the earthen tumblers that Raggy fetched from the dining room.

Harry and Vinnayana fetched some goat milk which they sipped as we sat.

As he squatted on the jetty, Trea offered to fetch Harry a chair but he held up his hand in what he seemed to believe was a gesture of gracious self-denial.

'He has to manage every detail of his body,' Vinnayana said. 'The mind in touch with the fingernails.' Her voice was soft and persuasive but again there was a note in it which valued its own self-restraint.

'I find toe nails most difficult,' Raggy said solemnly.

Mild fun. I was the only one who smirked.

'Of course, they are furthest out,' Trea said, not acknowledging or perhaps unaware, I wasn't sure, of his ironic intention.

'I'm getting there,' Harry said, turning his back on us as he squatted and looked towards the waters of the lake and the setting sun.

'You see,' Vinnayana continued, 'the setting sun, the end of things, will cast long shadows. It is the renewal that Harry is striving for. That's why he's here. The body and the shadows that it casts, internal and external have to be aligned. They are most out of line when you reach the sunset of hope – the longest shadow.'

She was blinking gently as she spoke, as though she didn't care if anyone was listening. Raggy was. Intently, though he must have heard it, or something like it, a hundred times before.

'At noon, if you can choose the spot where the sun is directly above you, you will cast no external shadow. The darkness will be under your feet. You will be trampling on darkness. No bigger than your foot's print.'

'Wow!' said Raggy. 'Wow! That's it!'

Harry turned round to face us now, still squatting on the boards.

'I said a prayer to Surya who is leaving us for another night,' he said, grinning at his own playful profundity. I think he merely wanted us to know that he knew what the sun god was called in Sanskrit.

'Has it all helped with your cancer? Vinnayana tells me it's been miraculous,' Trea asked.

'I feel better than I have done in twelve years and the doctors in Poona, on our last visit, said the spread has halted. That's according to their old science. What we practise here is the new science. They've got the tools to tell you how sick you are, but don't have the cure. We do a combination of yoga, meditation, reiki, projection, magnet therapy, vibration and some stuff from the texts.' He looked to Vinnayana for help.

'Medical sutras,' she said.

'Long as it works,' Trea said.

Something shifted inside me. Trea's reaction was not cynical, not small talk, she meant it: 'Long as it works' – that which alleviates your suffering, to hell with science, to hell with intellectual snobbery, bypass all judgments about the intelligence of the believer, of the sufferer. It was an act of faith. Trea had been born a Roman Catholic but she wasn't religious. This was as close as she got: 'Long as it works'.

I found myself looking at her. Something stirred – the old feeling, an extension of wanting to protect her, look after her, to 'be decent' as she would say.

I think in that simplicity I saw what I hadn't seen before. An innocence in the pronouncement, a facing of life as it comes. A girl without guile or with such clumsy guile that it became its opposite.

Was that what she had been doing on the Internet, looking to face life as she found it? To make things, her life 'work' using anything at hand? But what had been at hand? Chat rooms and quick-meeting fixes and dating agencies that gave her a chance to find a man who was willing to talk in clichés and sympathize with her, go for boat rides and perhaps sleep with her?

Vinnayana – I could see as the sun went down, the shadows lengthened and the birds began gathering noisily to nest for the night, making a sound somewhere between an electric hissing and a subdued scream – had listened to Harry's little dissertation with the pride of a teacher. And then did I see her perusing my face and Trea's to see how much of it we had bought. Was there just the ghost of anxiety crossing her features, indicating that she knew Harry had been overemphatic?

'When Harry first came to me, I told him he had the explanations within himself. We all have. I could teach him nothing. What I *could* do is help release the energies that were locked inside him and which were probably responsible for the misdirected growth they call cancer,' she said. 'I keep telling him not to call me a healer. If he is locked, if the codes of his life have been stilted by the unconscious forces he has developed and stored like poisons in the spirit, then the new sciences have found the key. Release them, let them out.'

'You can't teach anyone anything. Not really,' Raggy said. 'I spent a few years in jail and thought they were teaching me to go straight. But I *was* straight. It was all of them who were bent. The judges, lawyers, jailers – capitalists, communists, the system.'

Vinnayana just looked hard at him. This wasn't her 'new world' discourse. His little attack on the 'system' was straight out of our college days. None of us had been to jail then, but we assiduously read Camus and Gide and Genet's *Thief's Journal* and constructed a fantasy of being the rebels who would challenge the undefined 'system'. Old talk.

Vinny was too young to realize that Raggy's banter was the teenage talk of the decade before she was born. That is when it struck me that she must be fifteen or twenty years younger than Raggy.

It was now dark and Harry began to chant to make his peace with the dark. Raggy lit candles and brought them onto the jetty, and when it began to drizzle and the rain started coming down harder, we retreated to the living room and opened the second bottle of wine and settled into the dusty, cushioned furniture.

'The night is for sleep,' said Harry. Not the greatest discovery in 'routinist' philosophy, I thought, but watched him bow in the same pseudo-Japanese fashion and retreat backwards to his bed.

Vinnayana stayed with us. Raggy said they were abandoning their bedroom and letting us occupy it; and it was Trea who said we would sleep in the room in which we sat. She insisted. Vinny agreed, probably relieved. She brought us sheets for cover. Trea said that she and I would find it romantic and give us the feeling of adventure. She was being polite. She didn't want to put our host and hostess out, but still the way she said 'we' would find it romantic, touched me. There had been no romance between us for the last six years. Yes, we fucked often enough, with her grasping the headboards of the bed and waiting for me to penetrate her faster and faster, concentrating on the friction that would make her come. It was routine, an exercise. Now she talked of romance but didn't throw even a glance towards me. Vinnayana was watching us.

We slept by starlight, the strange openness of the room towards the lake prompting memories and fears.

'I don't like her,' Trea said, turning over on her mattress under the sheet. 'I know she's gorgeous, I saw you looking at her in that way, but you wouldn't be happy.'

'Why are you so damned silly? I wasn't looking at her in any way. And the truth is,' I said, 'I think you are much more beautiful.'

'You're full of shit,' Trea said and turned and went to sleep.

Raggy brought us hot goat milk in the morning in the same clay tumblers. He was wearing a lungi and as we sat up on the mattresses on the floor, I told him what we were there for. He knew I was after his archive and he said that he had it. It was tucked away between the wooden ceiling and the solar panels of his roof – his storage space.

As we sat up, we saw that Harry was sitting at the far end of the jetty in a yogic pose, greeting the morning sun with a Sanskrit prayer. Good for cancer, I supposed, the rhythm of the earth and its rotation round the sun. Raggy showed me the Raj-era building photographs he had taken. He brought them out of his attic and didn't know till he opened the cardboard boxes that they had been eaten away by dampness and fungus, and whatever other predatory life infested his rafters.

We took the damp and partly destroyed photographs and spread them on the dining table and on the floor of the front room.

'Shit, they are fucked, man!' he said.

'Oh god, I'm sorry,' I said.

They were magnificent photographs, unique and precisely what I wanted for the TV series I was working on, called *Stones of the Ages*, a documentary on the architecture of India from early times through the British period.

Raggy bit his lip. He didn't seem devastated by the damage to his life's work. The negatives, he said, were gone, destroyed when he was in jail. He shook his head, taking more piles of photos he thought he had safely stored out of their now wet cardboard containers.

They had been left gnarled. Rats? The animal, or whatever it was, had chewed through a third or even half of some of them.

'You were going to give me money for these, weren't you? Your TV-wallahs? Screwed, man!'

'Of course,' I said as he spread more of the fragmented images on the floor and then on the dining table.

'So fucked, so nothing,' he said.

Vinnayana glided into the room and took in what we were doing. She was philosophical about it.

'Worms. The present destroys the past,' she said.

'Don't be so fucking clever, man,' said Raggy. 'It's my life's work.'

She wasn't slow to respond.

'If that's your life's work, honey, you've become a slave to the past and your own creative vanity, and now nature has taught you how important you are.'

She didn't turn on her naked heel and walk off. She stood there to allow him to swallow the correction she was used to administering.

Raggy looked at me, his expression that of a dog whipped in public.

'Shit, man, I'm sorry. That's what's left.' He shrugged. He didn't want to say anything to her.

'Can't some of them be saved? Can't you use bits of them,' Trea asked, 'and pay him?'

'I don't know,' I said.

Harry had finished his meditation and walked into the room now. He saw the fragmented photographs spread out to dry and immediately looked – with his obedient, searching, jowly face with its wrinkled skin and bags under the eyes – to Vinnayana for guidance as to how to react.

She knew he was waiting for her words and she spoke them.

'An attachment to the past, isn't it, Rajesh? In every sense. These pictures are of empire buildings, old temples, palaces, statues, the memory of decay. Now comes the *real* decay, to teach you what all this pomp and splendour is worth. And then your photography, the past which got you into fights and which made you betray your real – kind, good, spiritual – nature. Is it something you can't leave behind because you are the great snapper of snaps, the man with the eye in the eye?'

Admiration for the speech had made Harry's jaw drop.

'The balance of animal, material and environmental energies against human vanity is here to be seen,' she finished. What a flourish. Not a speck of sympathy. Trea looked at me.

'Hey, take it as a sign, Rajesh. Vinnayana is right,' Harry said.

And then Raggy exploded.

'I'll shove the balance up your arse, you Yankee son of a bitch!'

Trea intervened.

'No, enough!' She turned to Vinnayana and Harry. 'It's his work, don't run it down. It must have been a shock taking this stuff down and finding it destroyed.'

'I've got fuck all, man. I've got nothing. I don't know who's going to pay for the next bag of flour to make chappatis.'

'When's that been a problem?' Harry asked. He reached into a leather money bag attached to a belt under his lungi, drew a thick wad of thousand-rupee notes from it and flung them in the air.

'It's not a material problem,' he said. 'It's attitude, right?'

Vinnayana started humming, at first low and soft, and as the notes rose in the scale, louder. It was a Buddhist chant and she seemed to want to get into a trance. Which is what she did. She hummed as she walked to the edge of the jetty with us watching her and then dived into the lake, still humming.

It may have been her way of diffusing a volatile situation, but we didn't wait to find out.

'Hey, maybe she's right,' Raggy said.

'We should go,' I said, turning to Trea, and in a few minutes were in the car where the driver awaited his orders. Before we could get in and drive off, Raggy came running. He had three of the large prints which had survived to some extent.

'Listen, man, I've got nothing left. If I had even the airfare, I would have gone somewhere, done something. Look at these.'

I looked.

'You want these for filming in a documentary. Suppose the Daniel brothers or some other Raj artist had made sketches or watercolours of the precise buildings you want, from the angles you want, that would be even better than photographs, wouldn't it?'

'Yeah, it would be. But how am I going to get them to do

the sketches I want, apart from the small problem that they've been dead for a hundred and fifty years?'

'I'll paint these photographs, from different angles, man. Vinny wants me to put instruments away and work with my hands and eyes again. OK, I am a better painter than a photographer, I swear. I'll make them delicate, beautiful. Please.'

'Don't start saying "please" to me, Raggy. Do them and of course I'll use them.'

'If we caused any problem, Raggy,' said Trea, 'I am very sorry; and thank you for a lovely time. It's a lovely house. And I can't do it now, but say thanks to Vinny.'

I admired her for that. Where had this come from? A concern for other people's feelings? Not my Trea, not her style. Or had I been wrong all along?

It was six months before I saw Raggy again. I came back to India on another mission, dialled Vinnayana's mobile and was informed by an unctuous female Indian voice that no such number existed. I had a bad feeling about it. In the days after I left, I had struck a deal with Raggy on the phone. He was to deliver thirty of the paintings to me when I returned.

I asked Trea if she wanted to come with me on another trip to India but she said she was quite content staying at home and would even have the child over at weekends from boarding school because she missed her.

I had often thought of Vinnayana, her perky attractiveness and her formulaic, philosophical rambling. The surrender of sense, of the scientific centre of human thinking, to a nebulous and pervasive discourse of finger therapies, fantasies and the nonsense about 'energies' was, to adapt her language, a force-field of negativity around her. It repulsed me. It was Harry's recipe for survival and I pitied him – words, only words.

Trea, as though reading my mind, asked me if I often thought of Vinny and her raven-haired temptress' beauty.

I said I didn't. She was to me the Goddess of 'boogoo'.

Trea knew the word. It was from the private language that lovers construct, and meant all irrational New Age rubbish – religious and superstitious belief and everything indulgent, beyond the grasp of reason. 'Boogoo, boogoo, boogoo ...', as I had recalled to Trea, was a haunting sound from my childhood, when wandering gipsy tricksters would visit our neighbourhood with their caparisoned Brahmini 'magic' bulls decorated with bells and garlands on their horns. The gypsies carried strapped drums which they played with a bow against the taut skin. They would gather a crowd with the 'boogoo, boogoo' noise of the drum and when the audience had formed a circle around man and bull, they would ask the bull to predict the future. The gypsy would pick a blushing girl from the audience and ask the bull if this girl was married. The bull would shake his head. The audience would be amazed. Then would come the enquiry whether she will be married before the year was out. The bull would shake its head again and ring the bells in its horns. 'And next year? Will she be married and find happiness next year?' The bull would nod its head emphatically, several times. The crowd would applaud. The blushing girl would hide her face in her hands. The drum would speak 'boogoo, boogoo, boogoo' and the gypsy women and urchins would gather contributions from the crowd.

There'd be more questions from the master gypsy. Would the cyclist who had stopped to watch the show travel abroad next year? What class would the young student score in his exams? The bull would answer by pawing the ground or shaking and nodding its head.

Vinny's prattle was a sophisticated version of the gypsy's trademark sound. Boogoo, the music of our deep irrationality.

And still I kept Trea's 'Long as it works' in mind.

I drove a Land Rover myself this time, and reached the forest lake-house by night. I had had no phone contact but decided to take the chance. The crickets were in full-throated splendour and the dark house was silhouetted against the night sky. My heart sank. Was I on a wild goose chase? The drive had not been easy, but at least I knew the way.

I got out of the sturdy, dusty vehicle and walked to the side of the building, and saw to my relief that there were three candles burning in the bedroom which had a casement window to the side. The front door was open and I walked in, calling out.

'Rajesh? Raggy? Vinnayana?'

There was no answer. I was in the lake room and passed through the curtain to the room in which I had seen the candles. Raggy was there, slumped in his wooden reclining chair with the candles burning on stools and on the central table. He must have heard my shouts but hadn't stirred. He said nothing even now.

'Raggy? Are you all right?'

He sighed. No surprise at seeing me.

'No,' he said. 'The bitch left me. They've gone.'

He lifted a bottle from the floor and took a swig from it. I followed his arm down as he replaced the bottle carefully next to him. There were several empty bottles lying on their side, casting shadows on the jagged brick floors.

'What the fuck has happened to you?'

'What happens to all of us,' he said. 'She's gone with Harry. She's run away. He has millions and his smart lawyers got her a divorce and they got married in New York.'

There was only the bed to sit on, so I sank down on it. The place smelt damp and of alcohol. Raggy was drunk but coherent.

'I don't believe it,' I said. 'Wasn't he married?'

'We ... she ... knew he was divorced and his sons used to send us messages on the phone hoping that "Pappy" was better, but really wishing he was dead. Her reiki worked so well that he felt better and started fucking her, and when I found them, they made a run for it.'

A silence descended on the room. I wanted to say I was sorry, but the whole situation struck me as incongruous, so I said nothing. He passed me the bottle, but I declined.

'I know you're thinking you should go and leave me to wallow, but don't go. Stay at least till tomorrow. I shall be sober. I'll go for a swim tonight and be clean. And your paintings ... I have started them.'

'Go for a swim in the morning when I can sit on the jetty and watch you, or when I can swim too.'

He laughed. 'Thank you, old man,' he said, but the appellation reminded him of the real old man in the game and he let out a short, sneering laugh.

We talked into the night. He did most of the talking, rambling and bitter about how he had introduced Vinny to ideas of freedom. She had been brought up in a strict lower-middle-class household and it was only when he took on an assignment as a favour to a friend who was ill and went to her college to photograph the graduates and the graduation ceremony that he met her. He was reading a book on Gaia and he made her hold it as a prop as he photographed her under the watchful eye of her possessive parents.

He was going to get the next graduate girl, his next photographic subject, to hold the same book, but Vinny objected. How could he do that? Use the same prop for all the girls? Everyone would know it was a photographer's prop and that the girls weren't really reading a book about Gaia, whatever that was.

'But it *is* a prop,' Rajesh had insisted.

'Not any more. Find something else. Give the next candidate a fan or a feather or something, I am keeping the book and reading it,' she said.

It was bold. Very bold. And it got him interested in her to the extent that he sought her out and, many books and clandestine meetings later, they eloped. Her parents disowned her and he now told me that when the photography assignments dried up he even committed fraud in order to feed her and keep her happy. She had been a chemistry graduate and her parents wanted her to go on to study medicine, but she went another way. By the time he emerged from jail, she had become a student, proponent and practitioner of all that she now 'knew'. The institute in which she had enrolled began to post what they called a progressive understanding of cancer on the Internet. They never claimed they could cure it, but they did say they could dissolve its reasons for assailing the body through purifying the spiritual energies that governed its functions. Cancer was not their sole claim. They could tackle most ailments.

Vinnayana, with her sharp brain and ability to devour English books, became the chief philosopher of this counter-cancer theory and began, Raggy said, to develop techniques from the new sciences which could be applied clinically as therapy.

'But did you ever believe it yourself?' I asked

'Of course. It is bound to work,' he said, with an insistent vehemence. He didn't sound as though he was trying to convince himself, but there was a register of falseness in the assertion.

We went to bed in the small hours of the morning. He struggled out of his chair and showed me to Harry's room with the narrow trestle bed now pushed from the centre of the room to the wall.

Having slept two or three hours, Raggy was awake at dawn and I heard him splashing into the lake.

He came dripping into my room with a cup of tea for me. He was carrying an ordinary china mug. I sat up on the edge of the high bed, my legs dangling.

'I thought tea was banned,' I said. 'And real mugs?'

'Balls to all that,' he said. 'I got a gas cylinder and stove.'

'All discipline is self-discipline,' I said.

'You saw the whisky bottles,' he said and smiled. 'I've cleared them up.'

He gave no sign of being hung-over, which I certainly would have been if I had gone through the amount of liquor he swigged even after I got there. He seemed to know what I was thinking.

'Miracle waters. They clear up hangovers,' he said.

I sipped my tea.

'Have a dip. Jump in and out. There's a towel on the jetty; and then I'll show you the paintings. Only two, but all this has held me up, stopped the work, you know?'

I had a short swim. He cooked some eggs. The dining room now housed a fridge which worked on gas. He took some chappatis out of the fridge and toasted them on the stove. After we ate, he showed me the two paintings. They were delicate, exquisite, startling, and were better for my televisual purposes than the original photographs.

'They look like they're really old,' I said.

'Just a technique, plus treating the paper,' he said. 'Trade secret.'

One was the interior of a temple he named and the other of an old British house on the banks of the Hooghly in Calcutta. 'They are fucking beautiful,' I said. 'But this house, surely it hasn't been maintained. I've been to Calcutta and the old buildings there are falling down.'

'Sure, sure, no, I restored them in my imagination, which is what I thought you wanted. Made them look like they were when they were built.'

'They are fucking beautiful,' I said.

'Yeah, pity about the fucking,' he said.

I thought I knew what he meant.

'I'll need twenty or thirty of them, though,' I said.

'I have all the time in the world. Just do me one favour; take me to the village and back and I can order some stocks.'

I stayed five days. Once or twice, Raggy disappeared into the trees behind the building. The second time, it was while I had consented to do the cooking and was looking for a can opener. I shouted to Raggy and noticed that he had stepped out.

I followed him down the path through the trees and at some distance heard him talking to himself. I couldn't hear the words but could make out that he wasn't talking in English or Hindi. It was Kannada by the cadence. He would stop and then speak again, as though he was having a phone conversation. He had told me that he didn't communicate with anyone because Vinny had taken her phone with her. I had offered him my phone if he needed it, but he waved the offer away. He didn't need to talk to anyone, he said. So was he muttering a faltering, secret prayer to the bushes and trees? I didn't go any closer to find out. It was none of my business.

I ran back to the house and took the saucepan off the stove. The can of aubergines could await his return.

He came back with an armful of kindling for the fire. He chatted away about gathering only dry twigs, to convince me that that was the mission which took him away from the house into the thickets.

We ate by the lakeside. Then we drove to the village for supplies.

My mobile phone rang as we drove. It was Trea and she was sobbing. She said she had tried to get hold of me. Why was I out of range?

'What's the matter?'

'You have to come back,' she said.

'I am deep in the country, but what's wrong?'

'Everything's wrong,' she said.

I stopped the car because she was gasping for breath between sobs. She said she couldn't tell me on the phone and I was to come back. I said she had to tell me or I would be worried sick.

'Oh what can I say, you'll kill me,' she said.

'No I won't,' I said. 'You know you can say anything you like to me. That's our tryst, isn't it?' Of course it wasn't, but that would make her feel comfortable.

She tried to stop crying. She had met a man on the Internet six months ago and they had exchanged photographs and the sort of information or lies that people do, and he said he was coming over from France just to meet her. They arranged to meet in a hotel in Whitstable. She had booked the hotel and waited for him. He came by car and turned out not to be the man in the photographs but a brute who raped her.

'Why did you go into a room with him?' I was shaking with shock and anxiety.

'I didn't,' she said. 'I met him outside the hotel and when I saw him and he identified himself and started grinning at me, I knew I had made a mistake. I spoke to him for ten minutes to get rid of him and then left; gathered my things and drove back home. I don't know how he managed to follow me, but he did; and then, yesterday, he came in from the back door which we leave open and attacked me.'

'He raped you?'

She didn't reply.

Yes, she had been to the police after he had driven away. She had been too afraid to resist. He was huge and he had his hands round her throat. She obviously didn't know his real name, but she got the car's number plate. That was no good because the police found it abandoned in a railway station car park. He obviously wasn't from France.

I said I would start my journey back straight away. Where was she?

She said she had two friends staying over and they would stay till I returned. The child didn't know. I said she needn't say anything to her.

It took me two days to get back to London and to Trea who now revealed to me that she hadn't been raped at all. No, it wasn't all a lie. Everything had happened as she had told me, but she had fought the man off and he had limped away when she kicked him in his crotch and ran out of the house to try and get to the neighbours'. She had been to the police and two policewomen had come round and taken whatever details she could remember from her.

Why did she tell me that she had been raped? I didn't ask, but she answered anyway.

'I wanted you back. I miss you,' she said.

That was it. For months after that, I put my work and Raggy and the paintings out of my mind, till the TV project came up to its deadline and to the point of completion.

The crews were out in India and they were now clamouring for the pictures. I had to get to the shoot and again proposed to Trea that she come with me as I would be away a few weeks. The child would be with Trea's mother and stepfather in Ireland for the summer holidays and she could do her own surveys for her oriental art business while I was working.

The monsoon was late that year and it rained very heavily during the end of July. The jungle was lush and green as we drove to Raggy's house. There had been no communication with him. There was no way to talk to him except a postal address to the nearest village post office from where he said he would pick up his mail and send letters out. I had written him a card but didn't expect a reply.

Torn off the hinges and battered by the wind, the front door was hanging from its jambs. We ran in the pouring rain from the Land Rover into the house which was dark with thunder clouds obscuring the daylight. The rain didn't pour into the open front room, but it beat a tattoo on the dark surface of the lake. Previous rains had done their damage to the house. It seemed as though a flood had soaked the front room. The lake had come over the jetty and the flood seemed to have been high enough to sweep over the raised foundation and floor of the house. It looked like a strong flood which had dashed the furniture against the farthest wall and spread a layer of streaked mud all over the floor. The house looked unlived-in rather than destroyed.

'He didn't think of floods when he built it?' Trea remarked.

'It's not all that bad. It can be cleaned up,' I said. 'Doesn't look like anyone's been here for days.'

'He might have been driven out by the flood,' Trea said. 'He'll come back.'

'No, it looks like he went off before it,' I said. 'The mud has actually dried out.'

I searched the other rooms. Raggy had left no clothes but the junk of their simple living – the pots and pans and earthen mugs, the brooms made of branches that Vinnayana had made her cult of 'wholeness' – were still there.

A disgust for this place came over me. It was hollow; a shell woven out of the spittle of deceit. A delusion. People fooling themselves.

'I want to get out of here,' I said.

'The roof's not leaking. We can hang about till the rain stops,' Trea said.

'No, we go now,' I said.

We did, and drove back to Bombay without stopping. It took us eighteen hours of desperate driving and driving against truckers who came at us with their blinding headlights. Trea didn't like it. She screamed and shouted and fought and tried to wrest the steering wheel from my hands and even bit me in the arm when I told her that I was in the driving seat here and she should shut the fuck up.

From our Bombay hotel I called the several crews filming the material for the series and told them there had been a bit of a hitch, but they were to continue. We wouldn't be able to use the pictures perhaps, but we'd find a way of doing the films without them. I told them to research and interview the country's architects and architectural historians. They said they had it covered.

Trea had become sulky since she bit me and drew blood. I wasn't thinking of her. She'd quieten down. We had booked our flight and were packing to go when Trea's mobile phone rang.

'It's Raggy,' the voice said. He asked for me and Trea gave me the phone.

'I know you're going this evening. I'm sorry I wasn't there and you made that trip into the wild for nothing, but the place flooded and I had to leave.'

'Where are you?' I asked.

'Doesn't matter. I can get you the thirty paintings the next week. They're done.'

'I'm leaving now,' I said. 'Is there any way you can get them to my director? He'll be in Bombay in a few days.'

'I can do that. Can I have the cash for them, though? In currency, not a cheque, I'm afraid.'

'I can arrange that,' I said.

'Listen, I know this is unusual, but can you give me the money in pounds sterling?'

'Let me see.'

'And you don't have to send the paintings back to me in India. I am lending them to you as per the contract you mentioned, to film them with a rostrum camera or whatever for your purposes, and a friend of mine will collect them from your studio in London on the same day. Is that okay? He'll identify himself and give you a code number which I'll tell you now so you know it's the real guy.'

'Okay. And yes, I can get you the cash in sterling.'

'Give me your director's name and phone number and I'll get in touch,' he said. Then in a whisper he gave me the five-digit code which his man would use to collect the paintings.

'Got it. My director's name is Peter. He'll be returning with the crews in four or five days, so get them to him. And then pick them up in England, yeah?'

'Sure, I can do that,' he said and then wished me well and rang off.

'How did he get your phone number?' I asked Trea.

'I think I gave it to Vinnayana last time,' she said.

'But she's in the US.'

'There are phones and e-mails there, you know,' she said.

'I wasn't thinking how, darling, I was thinking why.'

'Don't call me darling,' she said.

We got back to London the next day. As I got to my office at the TV channel, my secretary told me that the director of programmes would like a word.

I went to her office for the 'word' which would, in her straight-to-the-point way, be almost just that.

'How was the trip? I heard about your photographer and the paintings not being ready or something?'

'Sorted,' I said. 'Peter's bringing them. I'll shorten the edit, work night and day, and we can start broadcasts on India's Independence Day – 15 August.'

'Tight, but go away and earn your living,' she said, grinning in her endearing way. 'But did you have a good time? What about this photographer who lives in the jungle? I told the boss about it and he said it sounds like *Heart of Darkness* and you journeying into the jungle to find Mr Kurtz.'

'It's worse than that,' I said.

Peter returned with the paintings and we started work on them immediately.

'You gave him the money?'

'Not before the contract was signed,' he said.

'What did you think of him?'

'Old hippy. Shifty.'

'Yeah, but the work, I mean it's like some nineteenth-century master.'

'Yeah, it's good. And he's used some art school forger's technique to make the paintings look really old.'

'They were going to be photographs, but they were destroyed. But this is way better.'

'I agree,' Peter said.

A young man – Raggy's cousin, apparently – took the paintings after giving us the five-digit code.

The next day, someone who called himself 'an Indian collector' phoned my office.

'Sir,' he said when I'd identified myself, 'you have smuggled my paintings out of India, disguising them in a camera package and paying bribes to customs. I have found out. I can have you arrested.'

'Who the hell are you?' I asked.

He identified himself by name and said he was one of the most diligent and well-known collectors of antique works. He volunteered the information that he was not very rich but had done this all his life and that Rajesh, posing as a photographer who wanted to use the paintings for an assignment, had stolen the paintings from him and disappeared. The police were on the case and now they knew that they had been smuggled out in the equipment of a British film crew. That's how he had traced me after a series of phone calls. I knew that the paintings had been transported with the equipment of the crew and couldn't argue with him on that point.

'But aren't they his own paintings?' I asked.

'Yes,' he said, 'and I am Chiang Kai Shek! Sir, you know nothing about Indian art. These are original Raj paintings by Carmichael, Carpenter and Doyle. They are worth thousands and thousands. Did you for one moment think they were the work of this fraud? Or this century?'

Of course I felt like a fool. The man was telling the truth.

He said he wanted me to turn the paintings over to him and I had to tell him that I had passed them on, back to Rajesh's agent in London.

'That is criminal! You will be hearing from me.'

I tried to persuade him that I was an innocent party. I sympathized with him and said that if he could prove he owned the paintings, we would pay him for their use, and would try and help him retrieve them. But he was far from happy and hung up with a threat.

Things fell into place. Not the least a feeling of having been made a fool of. In retrospect, the fabric, the paper or card on which the paintings were could not have been early twenty-first century; there had been no sign of painting activity in the lake house. The painters I knew were always at work and always littered their studios. And the phone call from the forest?

I told Trea.

She laughed.

'I knew there was something fishy about both Vinny and Raggy and all that set-up with reiki and crickey!' she said.

'Then why didn't you tell me?'

'Someone should have told Harry,' she said.

'But you said "Long as it works"!'

'Sure. But not for him. It was working for them, wasn't it?'

'You knew that there was ... that Raggy and the woman were in some kind of scheme?'

'Plain as bloody daylight. I know you think I scour the Internet for men, but I spend most of my time looking up the symptoms and cures for the illnesses I imagine I have. And this woman, the one whose boobs made your eyes pop out, doesn't know anything about reiki, about magnet therapy or anything else. She's learnt to talk convincing nonsense, and that's about all.'

'But you don't believe all that stuff, do you?'

'Of course not. But, I sometimes think I have blood cancer and sometimes that my lungs are packing up, and then I look for anything that works. Even boogoo.'

She grinned because she had used my word.

'What illnesses?'

'No illnesses,' she said. 'Hypochondria. That's what I've got. I looked up the cure for that on the Internet.'

'And you're cured?'

'Didn't try it. It was all psycho-boogoo. You know what I'm glad about?'

My silence invited her to say.

'That we never planned anything with that sort of closeness.'

'Planned what? To play some stupid game living in the jungle? Why do you call that closeness?'

'It was obvious he was part of the game, using her magic treatments on Harry when he knew it was hopeless.'

'Not so obvious to me,' I said.

'No good prescribing specs for the blind,' she said. 'You know you're an idiot.'

I kissed her. We made love that evening after she had wiped out a bottle of white wine. But this time something had changed. It was as though whatever she had realized about Raggy and Vinny had brought her closer to me.

It was a month before the collector called again. Because of what he had told me, our lawyers had said I might have to suspend the series. I had tried to get in touch with him, but hadn't recorded his full name or his phone number. My office had tried all the collectors in Delhi and Bombay but to no avail.

'I'm very glad you called. We owe you some money.'

'Damn your money,' he said.

He had traced Raggy. He and Vinnayana were living in LA in a huge house that belonged to her former husband, a fellow called Harry. They had even inherited a vineyard from him and were now selling his designer wine. Rajesh was even now, he said, trying to sell the stolen paintings to the Indian billionaires of Silicon Valley.

'And Harry?'

'Dead. A week after marrying her,' the collector said. 'Galloping cancer and he had all the drugs, but went to India and threw the medicines away. He lost his chance for a little more time. Now she is married to Rajesh and he has applied for an American passport. She is already registered. I believe this girl and Rajesh were married before and got divorced and are now married again! Strange people, eh?'

'Hmm ... using boogoo,' I said.

'I am not following, sir,' he said.

I didn't attempt to explain.

'I've got my detectives on them,' the collector said.

'So they inherited everything from this fellow ... Harry?'

'No, no, his sons are fighting them in court. But your friends have taken all – two big houses, swimming pools, bank accounts, everything. Harry made the wills in her favour, calling her goddess or something.'

'Yes, he was made to believe he was having a miracle cure. But, sir, where did this Harry make his money?' I asked. 'Out of wine?'

'No, no, the same company your friend and his wife have now taken possession of. They are directors.'

'What company?'

'This multinational chemical company that manufactures and sells drugs to fight cancer. They have monopoly because of new research,' he replied.

TWO

bollox

From: gajan69@rediffmail.com
To: projectfinance@hotmail.com

Dear Mr Crookshag,

Forgive me for interfering like this. This letter is about your most fortunate find of my cousin who is to donate his parts to you through the Wholebody organization. May God bless the transfer. Of course we know that we are not supposed to get in touch with you, but I am doing so for a very particular and religious purpose.

My cousin was definitely told when he signed the papers for Wholebody that he would have no contact with the receiver of his parts. The match for everything, tissue and all that, would be done anonymously and the donor and receiver would never know who is who. We know why the best way is this way as there can be no questions asked afterwards. We are still wanting everything to be done through Wholebody itself, but there are some facts which I feel are tending to cause my cousin to withdraw his offer. They are to do with our spiritual beliefs.

I must put it plainly, Mr Crookshag. In our religion we would not mind if the kidney or the heart were donated to someone who is a stranger, but in the particular part that demands transplant due to your unfortunate accident is the seat of all energy and procreation according to our holy shastras. Power passes from it from one generation to the other. It is the seat of shakti, producing the juice of life; and all of our sect and my family are feeling that we must know to whom this vital instrument of the life-giving source is passing. In whose body the life-making organ of my cousin will come to rest.

You must be knowing the idea of spirit and power passing from one body to another, like Buddhists believe in spirits living in different people one after the other. We are not Buddhists but orthodox Hindus with tantric tradition deep in our family past, and though nobody in the family has ever donated the organ to someone else's body before, we have taken saintly advice and know that it is like passing on life-power to another person.

Naturally, we want to know that this life-power is passed on to a good man and we are confident that Wholebody would have found good and deserving people for receivership.

I would request you only that we may know something about you before my cousin can travel to Dubai for the operation. I hope this is not taking you too much by surprise and wish for speedy conclusion of your unfortunate state of affairs.

Your friend,

Gajan Nath

From: projectfinance@hotmail.com
To: gajan69@rediffmail.com

Dear Mr Nath,

How did you find my official e-mail address and my name? By the way, it is spelt Cruikshank and not as you addressed me in your mail. I take this breach of security very seriously and will sue the company for betraying the anonymity I was assured of in the contract. Something for which, may I tell you, I have paid a considerable sum.

Yours,

Cru.

From: gajan69@rediffmail.com

To: projectfinance@hotmail.com

Dear Mr Cruikashokh,

Sorry for misguiding your name. I will tell the secret. We paid the Mumbai doctor who was hired to carry out the tests on my cousin for blood and tissue type to ask the private clinic in London and find out who the budding receiver of our organ was going to be. He charged us a lot of money for finding out. He assured us that my cousin's types in blood and tissue and a few things in his DNA are very different and rare and so it is God's miracle that they have suited and matched yours. I know it is the hand of Bhagwan that has brought my cousin to your salvation. His organ is tried and tested as he has three children. Three more were also there, but one died of typhoid fever and two of TB.

You seem to be a very good, proud gentleman, determined about the spelling of your name and everything. As I said, we would still be not happy to go through all this without knowing to whom we are giving the life-force.

Your friend,

Gajan Nath

From: projectfinance@hotmail.com
To: gajan69@rediffmail.com

Dear Mr Nath,

I appreciate the ideas and sentiment that your religious tradition perpetuates in you. Oh dear! How am I to say that I am a worthy receiver of the life-force! Let me just say that I am to marry for the second time and the young lady to whom I am engaged, though of contemporary thinking in every other way, has not reconciled herself to the fact that we may not have a child by natural means.

I don't know if you know my circumstances, but owing to an unfortunate accident at first and then a hereditary growth, I have had amputations of the organs in question. Though the operation is very rare, the specialist from whom I sought treatment is sure that the transplant will restore my ability to procreate. I have been waiting for years for the correct match to be found, and both my fiancée and I were delighted that one had been.

Your communication came out of the blue. Yes, of course we shall respect your sentiments and shall answer any questions you would like to put.

Ever,
Cru.

From: gajan69@rediffmail.com
To: projectfinance@hotmail.com

Dear Mr Crookshark,

Thank you very much for agreeing to the answering of all questions.
I want to convey to you that we are very poor in our family. In fact, I
am the only earning member and supporting my cousin and his family
also now. To settle the cost of bribery to the UK clinic and the greed
of the Mumbai doctor, can you please help with sending me directly
three hundred pounds sterling? This will cover everything.
I know you will not refuse.

Your friend,
Gajan Nath

From: projectfinance@hotmail.com
To: gajan69@rediffmail.com

Dear Mr Nott,

Believe me, I have paid in advance and will still be paying a
considerable sum to Wholebody and have set aside a budget from
my limited funds for the operation and the recovery, etc. Your
demand, while entirely reasonable, must be the last. How shall I
send the money? And after that is done, can we proceed to inform
Wholebody, without any reference to this correspondence, that your
cousin is ready for the operation?

May I ask one question? If two of your nephews or nieces died of TB, is there any vestige of it in the family? Has your cousin, whose name you haven't told me, ever suffered from the disease and, if he has, in which part of his body?

Ever,

Cru.

From: gajan69@rediffmail.com
To: projectfinance@hotmail.com

Dear Mister Cruukskunk,

Don't send money. A broker of such affairs will come and fetch it from your office if you will supply the address by next e-mail.

As for the TB, yes my cousin was having TB but in his lungs and it was treated successfully. Thence you are getting a clear certificate of health from Wholebody.

Please tell us what your professional and religious leanings are.

Your friend,
Gajan Nath

From: projectfinance@hotmail.com
To: gajan69@rediffmail.com

Hi,

The address from which your agent can pick up the cash is 37, De Lancey Close SE 21 3HB. It would be most convenient if he can call after office hours.

I work in the city in a brokerage firm and my religion I suppose is Christian Anglican, though I would not call myself devout. I am a believer and probably believe with Mahatma Gandhi that all religions converge in a belief in God. Is that not what he said? I have got a book on tantric belief out of the library and shall make it my study immediately. I hope these answers are satisfactory. Can we now progress to fix dates?

Ever,

Cru.

From: gajan69@rediffmail.com
To: projectfinance@hotmail.com

Dear Mr Crutchshake,

You seem a very diligent person and myself and my cousin are well pleased with your attempt at finding out about our religion. I must mention that the most quick way for my cousin to be brought to the same medical centre in the world as yourself to donate his part is for him now to travel to Delhi and file an application for a passport, which he never knew of. Wholebody never told him anything about this arrangement and left it up to individual.

I have to sadly add that this trip and transaction to New Delhi, including bribes to expedite procedure of passport issue, will cost a small sum of money. Very large for us but cheap for you. It will be about £1700 more. We can ask Wholebody to put up costs but I fear they will be refusing. As soon as the money reaches through the same channel, we will be in swift transaction to Delhi. I will have to go myself as my cousin is a simple person and doesn't know much bureaucracy.

Your good friend,

Gajan

From: projectfinance@hotmail.com
To: gajan69@rediffmail.com

Dear Gajan,

I do understand that a passport is necessary, as I have declined to have the operation in India. I have engaged the best surgeon in a reputable and hygienic clinic, which will assure success and will be best for your cousin too.

This last time I feel compelled to send the money.

Etc

Cru.

From: gajan69@rediffmail.com
To: projectfinance@hotmail.com

Dear Mr Crutchshake,

Very pleased to have the cash which arrived safely. We are thanking you heartily. What is your star sign, even in Western astrology terms?

Your loving friend,
Gajan

From: projectfinance@hotmail.com
To: gajan69@rediffmail.com

Dear Gajan,

I don't understand what my star sign has to do with anything. I have paid you considerable sums now and want you to inform me when your cousin will be ready to travel.

Etc.
Cru.

From: gajan69@rediffmail.com
To: projectfinance@hotmail.com

Dear Crookshaonk,

You are making serious mistake. Please forward star sign. My cousin is nervous.

Your best friend,
Gajan

From: projectfinance@hotmail.com
To: gajan69@rediffmail.com

Gajan,

It's Taurus.

Cru.

From: projectfinance@hotmail.com
To: gajan69@rediffmail.com

Gajan,

No word from you. Please inform me as to whether the passport has been obtained.

Yours truly,
Cru.

From: gajan69@rediffmail.com

To: projectfinance@hotmail.com

Dear Mr Crutchshake,

This is a very terrible situation. I have not disclosed what your star sign is to my cousin but I know a very bad fact. My cousin is a superstitious fellow, which I am not, dear sir. I have done my B.A. and am engaged in education.

My cousin has been told that Taurus and Aquarius are absolute taboo signs and he cannot give away his testicles to anyone born under those stars as he will suffer for it. Nothing will happen to the oblivious person who is to receive, but because the life-giving organ is to be taken into another being and life, we have to do these checks and now I am sorry to inform you that nothing is possible. When you send the certificate of birth that my cousin is wanting from you, it will be the end and he will close with Wholebody.

This is a very unfortunate ending to our friendship, Mr Crookshaky. Sorry.

Your loving friend,

Gajan

From: projectfinance@hotmail.com

To: gajan69@rediffmail.com

Gajan,

I cannot believe your last mail! Why can't you tell your cousin that I am of a suitable star sign and be done with it? I do have a copy of my birth certificate, but I can't see why the date should be of any concern to anyone. Can't I rely on you to say you have received such a certificate and that it says that I am Libra or whatever?

Please, this is very urgent. You have no idea how long my fiancée and I have waited for a suitable donor to be available, as fifty factors seem to be at play in the transfer. The transplant becomes urgent as our plans for the future depend on this procedure and the hopes we have built around it. Please?

Your friend,
Cruikshank

From: gajan69@rediffmail.com
To: projectfinance@hotmail.com

Dear Mr Cruikshank,

At last the right spelling has come. The fellows I get the mails written from are writing anything coming in their heads. This time I am writing your name myself.

I do want to help you. I think I have a solution. Please send me an authentic copy of your birth certificate.

All sorts of things are available in India which you do not have in the UK. I will get some very professional people here to duplicate the birth certificate with a completely different date while all other details remain same. You can even use this at the time of entry into the hospital in case my other relatives start their own investigation. I will then pass off this new certificate to my cousin and his astrological guides. Everything will be hunky dory. Please do not worry.

Of course there will be small charge from the forgery people.

I am hoping this puts your mind to rest. Give my wishes to your good fiancée.

Your friend,

Gajan

From: projectfinance@hotmail.com
To: gajan69@rediffmail.com

Dear Gajan,

The certificate has been collected by your agent who asked me for £800 to defray the costs of the alterations to the certificate. He told me that part of it would be used for transport to Mumbai and living expenses for you there, and some of it would go to the astrologer to keep him from examining and questioning too closely.

I hope this removes all obstacles.

Yours ever,

Cru.

From: gajan69@rediffmail.com
To: projectfinance@hotmail.com

Dear Mr Cruikshank,

Congratulations. Your birth date is now officially 15th of March and so you are a Pisces. Nothing fishy, which is a good joke between friends.

My cousin and his celestial advisor are both pleased and cousin is packing trunks for Delhi where a quick passport agent who has already taken money is alerted for us. Very soon you will have good news. My fond regards to your wife-to-be who will rejoice at this chance my cousin is making possible.

Your loyal friend,
Gajan

From: projectfinance@hotmail.com
To: gajan69@rediffmail.com

Dear Gajan,

This is a great relief.

Ever,
Edward Cruikshank

From: gajan69@rediffmail.com
To: projectfinance@hotmail.com

Dear Edward,

I am writing from Delhi where we are staying till we get the passport. A very unfortunate occurrence has happened. My cousin met his classmate who is in political service with the Communist Party (Marxist) and they had gone out drinking one day. My cousin doesn't drink any alcohol. He sometimes takes bhang, which is a cooling, intoxicating drink made out of milk and one Indian herb on festival days, but nothing otherwise.

This wayward communist friend made him say the truth about how he was going to foreign for a transplant donation and the fellow gave to him all sorts of political rubbish about the rich world in America and the UK buying up the bodies and souls of poor people in India. They came back to our lodgings and I was arguing with them about who would feed children, ideology or cash. The miscreant fellow has persuaded my cousin that if he goes to some woman that he knows who is foreign, he can get money from Holland to stop having any operation.

I fear my cousin is now fearing for his ball to get cut off. The communist chap is always at our lodgings nowadays. What to do?

Gajan

From: projectfinance@hotmail.com
To: gajan69@rediffmail.com

Dear Gajan,

I haven't heard from you for days. What's going on? What has the communist chap got to do with it?

Cru.

From: gajan69@rediffmail.com

To: projectfinance@hotmail.com

Dear Edward,

We are still in Delhi and rethinking some things. My friend here, the Comrade Sunit is definitely against the exploitations of Third World for body parts and this kind of Internet shopping for everything. He is a very persuading gentleman and told us that the filthy and lonely peoples of the West are looking for everything on the Internet. They are buying love like this. They are doing dating agency and buying sex for having some company. Women are shamelessly giving themselves for dinner and presents. Also these people are buying people's body parts. They have lost all self-respect and exchanging lust like animals, and now have come to capture our women and men or parts of them.

This is spiritually bad. It means that the West is having no spirituality in its pocket and is therefore running after the body and has to do colonialism of poor countries. They are buying our girls for marriage and sex from Internet chattings. They are taking kidneys and hearts like cannibals. The Comrade Sunit says, and my cousin is believing him like anything, that the East is vital and has what the West is wanting and now the West should start paying for it.

Don't you think he is a very wise man, this the Sunit?

Your friend,

Gajan

From: projectfinance@hotmail.com

To: gajan69@rediffmail.com

Dear Gajan,

Of course what Comrade Sunit says is partly true. But you are in education as you told me and you and I, as people without a communist axe to grind, should look at the whole rather than the partial truth. I agree that Sunit is a wise man and am not surprised that your cousin and you seem inclined to agree with him.

But think of it this way. You and I have made friends through this transaction, haven't we? Can't we put the West–East argument behind us and treat each other as friends? I hope that after all this is over, we shall be real friends. Since I don't even know your cousin's name and have never communicated with him, I don't have any channel of affection towards him, but my dear Gajan, I do seem to want to understand you better and I can predict that you are only half convinced by Comrade Sunit's strong arguments.

I have made myself vulnerable to you as all friends do sometimes. I have told you of Carolyn, my fiancée, and how she has this determined, almost Oriental fixation with having our own child and not through artificial means. It is close to your religious belief about not violating the life spirit.

I have only respect for the feeling, and that's why I have come so far.

Believe me, Gajan, this is my last chance. I am in my late fifties and my last wife, who was ten years younger to me did abandon me for someone she found – as Comrade Sunit put it – on a dating service provided by the Internet. She took our daughter with her. Comrade Sunit has obviously a great amount of knowledge. He is right that being part of the West I have worked hard towards gaining material comforts – I am still a struggling finance advisor.

But I neglected my first family and paid the price. Now I seek pure happiness with Carolyn and having registered with several agencies for this transplant have been given a chance by Wholebody and your generous cousin for a new life and some future with a family and a child.

Comrade Sunit also rounded his argument to you by saying that the West should be made to pay. Perhaps he is right. I have demonstrated my willingness to pay. As I said I want us to negotiate this as friends and therefore want you to come out of it as a happy and willing party. I hope when all this is over, you and I will still be in touch and perhaps can even meet. I want then for you and I to look into each other's eyes and recognize humanity there, not exploitation. Please ask your agent to get in touch with me. I have some little token which may help you understand that I am not an exploitative bloodsucker of the West.

And may I ask again? Can you yourself, who matter to me, keep an open mind to my simple argument?

Your friend,

Edward

From: gajan69@rediffmail.com

To: projectfinance@hotmail.com

Dear Edrood,

You have written the most persuading e-mail letter. You are quite right. I do see you as a friend. This the Comrade Sunit is clever but you may be even cleverer. The Lord Krishna says, and it is backed up in our holy tantric texts, that people can escape their class and caste if they perform certain rituals and good deeds. Yes, I can see the Comrade Sunit's point about you being West and we being East, but I am also mightily agreeable to your argument that certain sacrifices and actions can make people stand together on a plane of eternity, equal and tied to each other by chains of friendship. And on that plane, sir, there are no directions, no East and West and no above and below. Can you see that?

My agent has conveyed your generosity to me.

Thank you,

Your friend,

Gajan

From: projectfinance@hotmail.com

To: gajan69@rediffmail.com

Dear Gajan,

I see that we begin to understand each other. You say you are persuaded by my arguments. But the crux of the matter is can you convince your cousin?

I took Carolyn out to dinner last night. It wasn't a happy occasion. I told her how far we had got in our communications and I related Comrade Sunit's arguments to her. Believe me, she sympathized with the main drift of what he is saying, but she did shed a tear for the way in which this very argument could disrupt the lives of two people who only seek a little happiness.

Your friend,

Edward

From: gajan69@rediffmail.com

To: projectfinance@hotmail.com

Dear Edwad,

The Sunit fellow has got a stranglehold. There was big fight between him and me last night in the lodging when he was up to his old tricks and I was standing by your argument saying Western and Eastern could be friends. My cousin was getting persuaded when the bastard the Sunit started to resort to physical fighting. When the fight got bad and I pushed him, the Sunit fell on one of the partitions in this useless hotel and this same partition disjointed from its attachments and fell on a lady who was sleeping on the other side. The landlord of the sleeping house heard all the noise and her husband, a Sikh with long hair, came to kill us with a knife. The landlord kicked us out without refund.

It is a complete disaster. We have no money. The last you sent me I sent straight to my family and they are not having any way of returning it. So we are on the street. I am writing this from the Cosmos Internet Café and the only resource for some help is you, my dear friend. I can get in touch with agent's company in Delhi. I will be staying all night on a park bench or something. I will be going to them early in the morning. If you will do the needful and send enough money for us to live for a few days, I will be getting back with the passport to south. It will also help to separate my cousin from the Comrade Sunit who is a nasty influence. As you graciously stated early on, I am looking upon you as a friend. Who else to turn to in times like this?

Desperate times,

Gajan

From: projectfinance@hotmail.com
To: gajan69@rediffmail.com

Dear Gajan,

Your agent called with alarming promptness and I have done the needful as you put it. Hope it helps.

Edward

From: gajan69@rediffmail.com
To: projectfinance@hotmail.com

Dear Edwerd,

Cousin and I are in new lodgings thanks to you. I told him we should buy rail ticket and go home, but this the bastard Sunit has tracked us down by devious methods even though I didn't tell him where in the whole of Delhi we were going. He is now telling my cousin that the Holland lady will pay him. He is forcing my cousin to come on their side.

What to do, dear friend? I am hating the Comrade Sunit now.

Your pal,
Gajan

From: projectfinance@hotmail.com
To: gajan69@rediffmail.com

Hi,

What is the Holland lady willing to pay your cousin? Surely that's
the bottom line.

Cru.

From: gajan69@rediffmail.com
To: projectfinance@hotmail.com

Dear Edrewad,

Despite all my trials, my cousin is now saying that he will go with the
Holland lady who is the communist fellow's main attraction. She has
come to India to talk to all peoples about taking kidneys and things
for Western people just like in our case. She is making a film about
these things and the SUNIT, the snake, says she will pay my cousin
to be actor in the film. They are not saying how much. I know my
cousin too well. He will be going with high bidder, I bet.

Your friend,
Gajan

From: projectfinance@hotmail.com
To: gajan69@rediffmail.com

Gajan,

This is exasperating. What are we to do? What is your estimate of
the payment for appearance in the wretched film?

Cru.

From: gajan69@rediffmail.com
To: projectfinance@hotmail.com

Dear Edward,

Some light has dawned on the dark horizon. Forget the payment for
the film. Last night I went and had a drink with the Comrade Sunit
without my cousin. The truth is that the Sunit is frantically in love with
the Holland lady who is making the film and she is also encouraging
him by having surrendered herself after he gave her some ganja one
night. He is saying that she has resisted repeat performances but that
she really loves him and is playing very hard for getting. But because
the Sunit is in touch with my cousin, she needs him. She wants my
cousin to appear in the film tomorrow so only one day is left before
she returns to Holland but the Comrade S says that if we pay for his
ticket to Holland and give him some consideration, he will see to it
that my cousin is very disappointed with the Holland lady and the

film and all the rot he has heard and will come back in line for the operation. I know you will cooperate with this last step.

No time to waste,

Your dearest friend,

Gajan

From: gajan69@rediffmail.com

To: projectfinance@hotmail.com

Dear Ederwad,

The whole plan worked like clockwise. The Comrade S was happy with the money and took my cousin aside confidentially to see Delhi sightseeing. He very cunningly said on their trip that the Holland lady was a real bitch and wanted my cousin to first have the operation and then come for filming as a person who was already a victim of the great organ colonialism. My cousin was surprised as he was thinking prevention is better than complaint afterwards, but the Sunit told him that this lady thinks on film it would better if he could show his cut-off piece or where it used to be AFTER operation. The no-ball location. That way, more people would be pitying him.

My cousin got very furious and came back to me. I cunningly said that this was even more evidence of exploitation. They were wanting to make a film on what they think is horrible and now wanting to pay him for showing his disabilities. So my cousin is being persuaded to change his mind again and soon, I think, as I have bought tickets out of Delhi. We will go back home and inform Wholebody that passport has been obtained.

Actually I know that the Holland lady is loving the Sunit too much. The passport and ticket and everything has been bought for the Sunit to go to Holland and he is very happy that now his love with the Holland lady has been made possible. I am suspecting that he has a wife he has to leave behind and his conscience is prickling. He said in Holland he will start a Macdonald's franchise or something like that to make big money.

Your friend and facilitator,
Gajan Nath

From: projectfinance@hotmail.com
To: gajan69@rediffmail.com

Dear Gajan,

Wholebody contacted me today, in fact within the last half hour, and fixed the date of the operation. I want to thank you for all that you've done, even though you never seem to be able to get my name right.

Yours truly,
Edward

From: projectfinance@hotmail.com
To: gajan69@rediffmail.com

Gajan,

The operation was carried out five days ago as you probably know from your cousin with whom, of course, I have had no contact though I *do* know he was in a contiguous operation theatre.

Now I would like to take up the matter in hand. You probably think that I am a completely gullible fool and that you have taken me for a very long ride to the tune of several thousand pounds. I want to tell you that though I do not doubt the veracity of your basic story, the fact that your family is tantricly inclined and so on, I do happen to know that a forged birth certificate, even with her Majesty's seal on it, should cost in the vicinity of a few hundred rupees, a few pounds, certainly not hundreds or thousands.

I want you to know that I didn't for a moment swallow the whole of your story about communist ideological interference and for all I know you never needed to go to Delhi.

I naturally (who wouldn't?) played along and did nothing that would get the cooperation of your family withdrawn, allowing you to believe that you were dealing with an eager and naïve Englishman who had fallen into your extortionist trap. The truth is the opposite. I have lodged all your e-mails with my lawyer and have now sought advice. I shall threaten to sue Wholebody Enterprises for disclosing my case and address to you, and recover all the money that you have extorted from me. I realize that having got a little intelligence, you set about to exploit me. Well, you've met your match, Mr Gajan – a name which, no doubt, has nothing to do with your real identity. I am sure Wholebody will, when my lawyers get in touch with them, penalize your cousin and family by declining to hand over the whole sum that was agreed between him and them. They will possibly, and I hope they will, deduct what I paid your agent who arrived eagerly at my doorstep each time.

I might add that what you have done amounts to extortion and I can give the police a pretty good description of your agent.

I am writing this knowing that if I do not, I would feel foolish rather than grateful for the rest of my life and, of course, I am not sure that your agent and you, with your oily assurance of assistance and friendship, would not turn up again with more blackmailing demands.

God knows how, but I don't put it past devious devils like you.

You could, of course, volunteer to return the money in reply to this mail. You people may be poor, but I feel you have victimized me and my simple wish for a healthy body. I hope for your sake it doesn't come to criminal prosecution.

Edward Cruikshank

From: Mailer-Daemon@rediffmail.com

Your mail has been returned unopened. There was a fatal error in the address.

There is no such account as gajan69@rediffmail.com

The original message was received at Sat, 17 May 15:05:01 -0400 (EDT) from root@localhost

----- The following addresses had permanent fatal errors -----

gajan69@rediffmail.com

----- Transcript of session follows -----

... while talking to mx2.rediffmail.com.:

<<< 550 Requested action not taken: mailbox unavailable

JARVIS, JARVIS AND SON, SOLICITORS

13, Theobald's Grove
London WC 1

Dear Edward,

Glad to hear you are recovering and that the surgeon predicts success.

I have had an extensive correspondence in the last two days with Wholebody about the matter you put to me. They profess themselves puzzled and insist that no breach of confidentiality took place and that the whole procedure was routine. Your donor, they insist, was not Indian or of Indian origin and they have, reserving his confidentiality and entrusting it to me as a solicitor, made his name, address and particulars known to me. I can certainly confirm that he was and remains of European origin and has never travelled to India or anywhere out of Eastern Europe except on the occasion of the operation.

As for the party with whom you have been in touch and who has used some leaked knowledge to extract money from you, I can confirm that this is an Indian portal and the man was registered in India with an Indian e-mail address. As you know, he has abandoned the address and cleared off. Our best bet is the police. The fact that he found out that you were to have this operation could have been made known to the miscreants from several sources, including it seems, by your own admission, from Carolyn's hairdresser. Wholebody of course refused to refund any of the monies paid by you to them for the transplant and consider the matter closed.

We must meet and discuss the ramifications of all this when you are feeling better. Meanwhile, what shall I do about the police and 'Gajan'?

Yours truly,
John Jarvis

THREE

adultery

The bastards. Not one of them turned up. Maybe they never intended to. Maybe there were no such bastards. Maybe Linefeld was lying. Wouldn't put it past him. Got us there on the pretence that they were coming, that they had power and money and taste, 'a combination made in hell' he said and some wit added that if it was combined with generosity it would be a combination made in heaven and we cheered and drank our sixth pint. Bastards all, pretending to be twenty. The same dead beat crowd, some of them unable to spot a rhythm or a metric line if it turned into an express train and ran them down. The pretence of decades has made their faces clownish.

'Ah Sufi, did you finish that epic? Any takers?'

'I am still working at it.'

'Remind me what it's about,' says Linefeld. He knows perfectly well that I have been working up the annals of the Raj in verse. I consider the British foray into India the most important human adventure since the Roman unification of Europe. It has no poets to celebrate it.

'It's about your Jewish mother. I've got to the section where she has her first bastard,' I say and he makes as if to throw his beer at me, but Vernon stopped him. He shouldn't have. They all wanted it. A good beer-throwing fracas would have brought back old times.

Vernon says:

'Cage the lions, jail the kings
Free the poets,
Liberate the bird that sings.'

He's been repeating that fucking line for forty years.

'We'll put it on your grave but not in my anthology,' I say.

And they take offence. 'Your anthology? Who says they'll make you editor?'

They! What will they do? Who will they appoint? What do they want? Will they ever come? 'they' are always silent. There comes no sound but remote command from them!

Linefeld said they were notoriously late, these fellows from Faber he knew, and who had promised that they would be at this pub at this time to meet us, fete us, but no one came. The mysterious kept their mystery. At eleven I said, 'They probably meant a poetry anthology for the next millennium. They want us to wait a thousand years, but we mistook, as we always mistake.'

So we all drink to the next millennium. The licensee of the Chalice is new, but old Robert must have told him of our weekly riotous gathering there in the Seventies. Robert, RIP, sour faced Robert – and damn his Pernod-sipping soul.

'So admit you lied. Tell one truth in your life, Linefeld. You were lonely for the old boys so you sent off an e-mail shot, a lying one. I've got to catch the night train to Brighton now, you dog. There were no editors, were there? And no anthology, was there?'

Linefeld looked at us through his dimmed eyes.

'The truth is always what you make of it, Sufi. Yes, there was an approach to me. They were going to be here. He was after exclusive rights to our stuff. I talked up the Chalice Poets, they all know about us ...'

'No such group, no such people. All gone into the dark, the interstellar spaces.'

'Only two are dead,' I said. 'Mike of liver failure and that old fool Sigmund, of AIDS. At his buggering age. No shame.'

'All good versifiers,' Linefeld said.

'Immortality be yours,' I said and walked out. It was a two-minute walk to Waterloo. She'd be waiting. I didn't have to tell her it would be the last train. She'd know.

And she did. Joanna came walking through the carriages in Brighton and shook me awake and led me like Mary led her lamb to the car and drove me home. I had fallen asleep.

'So was it successful? Are you the editor of the great anthology?'

As though she didn't know. I had to tell her they didn't turn up. She wasn't surprised.

'Linefeld. You still listen to him? Isn't this the tenth time he has said that he'll get your poems anthologized and borrowed money on the strength of the hope?'

'Third or fourth time. Don't exaggerate.'

'And how much money does he owe you?'

'He is a poet, he doesn't consider them loans. He thinks of the money that changes hands as tribute or libation.'

'He is a dirty, scrounging bastard.'

'Joanna, that's the perfect description. I wish I had thought of the phrase myself. A dirty, scrounging bastard. Not a syllable out of place.'

'Did you spend all the money you stole from my purse?'

'Yes. I couldn't go there penniless and good thing too, because when Linefeld said the boys from Faber would foot the bill for drink and dinner, I began to have my doubts. The boys from Godot. That's it. That's what that stupid play means – Godot is a publishing house.'

'So it wasn't the great millennium anthology, it was the great millennium piss-up,' she says.

She tucks me in bed, bless her. The house is quiet. The African who bangs his bongos in the basement and then bangs his girlfriends all night, with even more noise than he does the bongos, is asleep or more likely dead, because he doesn't need much sleep and Joanna won't hear of throwing him out. The rest of the kids, the lodgers, they don't want him out either, because that would be racism. So I plug my ears and keep my mouth shut – but still my eyes can see. And to tell the truth, my ears can hear right through the plugs. They get very sharp when, lying in the dark, they anticipate the noises of arousal and then the sound of fucking: the sighs and grunts and whoops as I lie abed – as the Metaphysicals would have it. But nowadays I rarely lie abed with Joanna who snores all night, exhausted by her labours. I can hear the goings-on and the cries that can never be mistaken for pain but are so close to those of yielding slaughter. Do they turn me on? Yes. Now they are the only things that turn me on. Joanna has developed warts and there's nothing her doctor can do about them. He's tried to freeze them off, but they don't go and when my hands find them in the dark, my passion dies. Too many of them. If she had some substance on her, it would be fine. But she's thin as a rat's tail and that makes the sagging skin more prominent. I encourage her to eat, to flesh herself out to take up some of the slack, but she looks sad and her eyes go a bit watery and I fucking can't stand it, so I don't say anything. And I do nothing because nothing comes my way. I can speak, I am getting a little on the tubby side, and whereas girls would look at me and flock to me after poetry readings, just asking for it, this passion I had for Jo stopped me. I had a woman. The rest was flirtation. I never believed Jesus when he said just looking was adultery. That's like saying window shopping is theft.

I started a poem once, in response to a competition. I might have won. It was to write a poem on adultery. I started it off with:

'Adultery is what adults do.'

There were more lines, but Jo found it on the typewriter and laughed her head off. She didn't get past the first line though. Or maybe she did.

'What do you know about it? What you mean is "adultery is what courageous adults do".'

Was that a way of pushing me to it? Defying me? Asking me what she hadn't the courage to ask outright? What did I know about it? Had I gone with someone else in the time I had known her? It may have been a calculated laughter, but it stopped the poem. Her derision was enough, because I loved and respected her and that stopped me from experiencing the thing that I was required to write about. So I hadn't strayed. It had never come my way in that way.

Rage, rage, against the dying of the erection. Fat lot of good it'll do you. It's like poetry, rage does no good, inspiration is all.

Oh she was happy I went on the jaunt to the Chalice. Nothing will ever come of anything, and we, who have known so much, have grown used to that. And yet I told her, when she asked about my day in London, that I could never get used to the new decor of the Chalice, whose wooden benches have been replaced by soft sofas and the bar turned to pine, and the mould and mirrors have been replaced by cheaply framed 'paintings' of 'Now Artists' as the leaflet calls them – for sale at the outrageous price of £130 each. They are crap. Paintings of doorways and doorsteps in Ireland? Does one need this? The most I was ever paid for a six-page extract of a poem, and this by the *London Magazine* in 1976, was £28. And that was that. I offered them another instalment but no dice!

Bless him. He'll sleep tonight. He keeps himself awake to listen to Patrick and his girlfriend making love and he pretends he's not listening, but I know the rhythm of his breathing, which changes when he is ever so slightly excited. And he gets erections listening to them, and never now by touching or holding or looking at me. Kissing is out. Not for eight years now. I don't remember how one uses one's lips and what one does with the saliva, but I still have dreams about the passion of his kisses, when his tongue began in my mouth to describe, in its own thrusting, circling, caressing language what he'd like to do to me between my legs. Are these thoughts renewals of youth or just signs of getting old? How I fight against the crows' feet! Everything else I can stand. It's the wrinkles that spread like cobwebs under and to the sides of the eyes. No amount of creams and bracing formulae shall tighten that skin again. I saw a documentary – about face lifts called *Hollywood Knives*. A woman had her face transformed, the wrinkles taken out, the pouches excised, the sagging neck cut back, and all without visible scars. Thank god I don't have a sagging jaw. There's nothing much to sag, the Adam's apple gets a little more prominent, but Sufi always said he liked that. He wrote a poem to my Adam's apple and he contrasted it with my clitoris, of which he said he'd made a study. But that was long ago, when love was new. And now I'm not so young or starry eyed, I know a thing or two ...

The men still turn and look at me in the supermarket, on the street. I can see their sly, not-wanting-to-be-discovered glances, but Tom, one of the wretched lodgers, axed that illusion too by saying that they were staring because I look a bit like that actress from a sitcom, the conceited one, and at first glance people are deceived. But if that was really the case, then why don't women look at me as much as men do? Because surely they are more sycophantic to celebrity and more addicted to envy than men? Tom didn't want to carry on the argument. He chivalrously conceded. Do the boys and girls feel sorry for me? No, I don't think so. I'm the landlady, Joanna the bill, Joanna the fresh laundry, Joanna the replacement keys, Joanna the moneylender, aunty Joanna. No, not shy Joanna, far from it.

And Sufi has to be woken up and showered and trotted off to his appointment. He might even get the wretched job. God give it to him. The kids brought the poster from the university, from their notice board. They concurred. It was just the thing for him. But their Uni used to be a Poly and Sufi scoffed at that.

'Me? Teach poly-dollies poetry? What next?'

But he's agreed to go and be interviewed at least. No tie, he said. A shirt but no tie.

'You don't possess a tie. And it would be false. I wouldn't want to falsify you.'

'Go out and fucking buy a tie for me,' he says. 'I am fed up of living my life on small vanities. That I don't wear a tie? Who the fuck cares whether I wear a tie or not? I used to think, I and the other anti-tie fools of the world, that we were changing it decisively – the world – delivering a blow for Bohemia. And finally one concedes that Bohemia is only the nasty part of the Czech Republic where they all wear ties. So get me a tie. The vanities will be banished. I grow old, I grow old, I shall wear a tie of tiger-stripes on gold. Get me a tie of tiger-stripes on gold, Joanna.'

I got a dark blue tie with a little self-pattern and he wore it. He trotted off and I went to the door and watched him. Down our crescent. 'The sea is rough today' is what I shouted and he didn't hear but he waved. Jacket and tie. My Sufi. The gulls cried as they do when Radio Four is trying to depict Brighton in one of its silly plays.

I tried to wake Sally, one of the girls on the first floor. We live on the ground and second, and the Kids, our lodgers, live in the basement and the first. That's the most suitable arrangement of rooms till we make enough money to block off their space from ours. But this way it's more lively and the large house is lived-in.

We sold up in Hampstead, West Hampstead really, four years ago and shifted down here. I was fed up of London and not having any money. The only thing I could do was run a house because when I ran away with Sufi, I quit law school. I defied my parents, so they left me nothing except the old family memorabilia; the house went to my older brother and now to his kids. I wanted a steady income. Something that Sufi never understood. The house we lived in was our wealth. Sufi had got a mortgage out on it when he was a schoolteacher in the dim past, in the sixties and seventies when he used to dress in kurtas and wrote pop lyrics and even strummed a guitar. That's when I met him.

And thank god he'd bought the house for some ridiculous sum from the landlord who was his friend and ran away on a whim to Cornwall to start an artist's colony. If it hadn't been for 33 Granta Gardens we would have been paupered by poetry.

'Roll me a joint and pour me some booze
I'm not going to cry
Or threaten to die
Tired of winning and happy to lose
Brown girls don't sing the blues...'

He recorded it in his voice, even though at the time it was before its time. It was intended for an Indian girl's voice – to sing in the hullabaloo of the swinging sixties. And there were no Indian girls singing and those who were wanted to be Carly Simon so no one paid any attention to Sufi's almost feminist songs. And of course he couldn't say he had written them because that would make them even more forbidden. Men couldn't write for women, not for real women. The sisters had to be doing it for themselves. Men could write for Lulu and Petula Clark, but not for the Asian Joan Armatrading. No, no, no. Not that there was one, though Sufi said there could have been if she'd adopt his songs – anonymously if necessary. But what could remain anonymous with Sufi? His advice to poets: pretend you're a train, stay on the lines.

Yes, Sally had done it again. Boring. She had taken too many pills in an attempt to kill herself. And of course she'd then set the alarm clock. Just in case. So Patrick and I dragged her out and ran her down to the A and E where they pumped her stomach out. The sight of her turned my stomach. I'd have to bring her back to life once again. The other kids all heard and came down and said the fellow who had ditched her was not worth the dirt on her trainers and Patrick said he'd fetch him back and make him lick them and she opened her eyes and said a good suicide was what she needed, she didn't want him any more. She had passed into the other world for a moment and now she knew that someone else was going to enter her fate. I said I hoped that that someone else would take responsibility for her bloody overdoses because I was fed up of this suicide lark and the other kids thought 'heartless

Joanna'. But suppose Sally had died? The Kids would have a good sentimental binge. Death. Great! What would I say to her parents? Her father an MP and her mum a GP and this silly Sally just a weepy?

I was fed up. Those mornings I could kick the lot out, close the house down and ... and Sufi wasn't even there to help. He was at his poncey interview with not a helluva hope of getting the job, so I don't know why I pushed him to it. Not that he would have helped with Sally. It would have been Patrick and me dragging her to the car anyway, but at least he'd have been home to let the guttering men in because the front wall of the first and second floors was going to collapse if the blockage and leakage went on and now there'd be no one here when they called, and you know builders, they come after three weeks when they say they'll be round the next day. Bloody Sufi, never there when he's required and always trying to sneak off to London. I bet Linefeld never even told him there was going to be an anthology. It was just a piss up. And he lied and went and stole the money I've earned with this wretched boarding house and frying organic eggs and organic toast and tea with semi-skimmed milk because these kids are mad and fussy and will take any number of ecstasy pills and poison themselves and then talk about bloody free radicals from burnt toast damaging their systems. Fools. Or 'the bastards' as Sufi called everyone. The hostile world, floating on illegitimacy.

Would be called William. Won't abbreviate it to Bill, oh no, that's not good enough for the poet, who will now struggle to find a rhyme for William when there are thousands for Bill and why? Because of course he'll put his name into a poem and make it the last word in the line for emphasis if you please. Spoilt William. Ridiculous William with blonde Rasta locks and a stud in his nose. Yuck and vomit as those pestilent kids would say. White man, blue eyes, black pretensions.

Couldn't resist it.

'I see you're a Rasta-Aryan,' I said.

'That's good,' he says. 'Never thought of it like that. William'.

'I am Mr Akhtar,' I said, trying to parody acting my age.

'I am very pleased to meet you, Mr Akhtar.'

And then we feel we have to turn to the third candidate out of politeness. She is a severe young lady dressed all in black.

'I have no name to offer. Just my presence and my poems,' she says.

'Suit yourself, Ducky,' I say. She bristles at being called Ducky.

The young man who calls us in for the job interview says it's going to be a joint 'deconstructive interview'. He congratulates us for getting to the shortlist of three finalists for the Poet in Residence's job and ushers us in. There are five people on the panel, two of them bloody college kids. A farce. We are seated in a semicircle. And William is asked to begin.

'I look on poetry as primarily an aural experience and interaction,' he says.

'Saves trees,' I say and the Chairwoman says my turn will come later.

William says his influences are Dylan, Eminem and the graffiti poets of New York. He has cut two Indy CDs of Rap and has his own web site.

'Ah Cobweb poetry?' I say.

The only one who laughs at this joke is William.

'That's cool, man,' he says. 'I thought this was supposed to be interactive, so Mr Akhtar can, like, interrupt, you know, no sweat, you know.'

'We'd rather he didn't,' says the Chairwoman solemnly.

The bloody kids are taking notes.

Then the woman in black. Prig. Thinks she's really so unassuming, when she's more assuming than a Gothic cathedral with fucking gargoyles. The course of lectures we are to give if we get the job is called 'Living Poetry' and she says, 'Poetry is not about living; it's about dying.'

Well she's close. It's about learning about dying by loving to live, I would have said. But it's not my turn.

'My subject is the valour of the human condition.'

Sort of right again, but I wouldn't have the cheek to come out with it. Like saying 'this is a penis' and yanking it out. Neither would I put it quite like that. Too solemn and cliched.

'From Beowulf to Wilfred Owen, the voice from the coffin.'

Talking of coffin, I started coughing. This woman was on target but not bullseye. The Chairwoman asked her questions and I could see that they all thought she wasn't a bundle of laughs.

Then the Chairwoman says, 'Your turn, Mr Akhtar.'

This is an invitation to shame. What
fifty-seven years old, doing the fuck her

I am on autopoet. I begin without w

'I have nothing to say about poetry. I agree wi..
Arnold that mechanical poetry is constructed by your wits
and real poetry is constructed in the soul. But I might add
that I don't believe in the soul, so I don't know where poetry
comes from.'

'That's sweet,' says William. The kids have stopped
scribbling. They wrote down 'Eminem' and the 'Graffiti poets',
but Matthew Arnold was a bit too much for them. I was in
the mood to push it home. I turned to one of them.

'You know what Keats said about poetry in that famous,
much-quoted letter? No, you obviously don't. Well, he said,
"Poetry should strike the reader as the wording of his own
highest thoughts, and appear almost a remembrance." Get
that "almost"?'

They didn't get the 'almost'. Except William.

'That is unique, man. Keats. Yeah?'

'The very same. But your Eminem doesn't appeal to me as
my highest thoughts, or Shaggy or these guys. It comes over on
the kids hi-fis all the time; it's the lowest common thought.'

'It is the voice of the people, though,' argues William.

'"Half a dozen grasshoppers under a fern make the fields
ring with their importunate chink. It doesn't mean they are
the only creatures in the meadow. Burke,' I say.

'Wow,' says William.

No doubt his openness to ideas impressed the panel and
they gave him the job. I knew I'd lost it when I caught the

...airwoman looking at the woman in black looking at me and wishing I were dead. I have never had such an awful look from anyone. The woman in black was thinking that I was the uncle who sexually assaulted her, the teacher who whipped her bottom in front of the class, the store manager who made her strip in public when she had only shoplifted one little bra she needed, the dirty old man's face at the bathroom window, the eater of babies, the sanctioner of suffering in India, the hypocrite priest who raped her sister ... not even someone as interesting as a serial murderer of children, an adulterer? An adulterer? A married man of lusts. A debauchee. Or was it the silly blue tie? If only Jo had listened and bought me one with tiger stripes on gold. We could have been employed today.

Sufi says he didn't take the job and deliberately sabotaged his own interview because they all looked very 'ageist' to him. They are only interested in appointing twelve-year-olds and none of them know the first thing about poetry. This is the first year they are running this course and it's only for the summer, for foreign students mostly and for people from the North who want to spend a few hard-earned weeks in Brighton and be pretend-poets and be in touch with real poets.

I tell him about Sally.

'Love kills,' he says.

'Then it's good we don't have any,' I say.

'I think you need a holiday,' he says.

'With what money? This guttering will cost whatever we've got saved.'

'I'll get in touch with KeyNote Christmas Cards again. They know me and trust me and they'll pay two pounds for each rhyme they take.'

'Kiss me under the mistletoe
One more drink afore ye go ...'

Or how about

'Bring out the turkey, be of good cheer
Like Christmas, I come but once a year.'

'If only even that,' I say.

He is hurt by the allusion to our not doing it and he hits back.

'Sell your Indian junk,' he says and goes upstairs.

'Why don't you take me to India. You say I need a holiday and you've been promising to take me back to your hometown for thirty years, Sufi. You are a liar and a dog. And a good poet,' I shout after him.

'OK, but with what cash?'

'I'll sell the Indian stuff,' I say. 'I'll go to London and take it to Sotheby's. We'll make a packet.'

'You can't sell your history,' he shouts now, alarmed that I just might.

'I won't, I can't, I promised my dad I wouldn't when I took it from our home.'

The shawls are more than a hundred years old and jewellery and exquisite statuettes, and the diary that goes with them of

Gannymede Mottram whom Queen Victoria appointed to be the keeper of India's archaeological sites. He was my great-great grandfather and a friend of John Lockwood Kipling, Rudyard's father whom Sufi calls 'locoweed' Kipling, after the ganja they probably smoked during the Raj. Anyway, he kept a journal of his doings. On the last page of the journal he had composed these lines:

Anne Mottram 1856–99
She who restored palaces
Across the land of Hind
Leaves all earthly vanity
And but this stone behind.

This was no doubt engraved on the stone in the churchyard in Behrampore. He had probably written it and Sufi's joke was that they should travel to India together in order to rewrite the epitaph on the headstone, so that it scans and rhymes. The 'Hind/behind' rhyme didn't work 'in aural poetry' he said – it only seemed to work on paper.

'And aural is the thing, or oral as in Clinton. Let's do the old girl a service, change her epitaph.'

And there are her sketches and paintings of the palaces. She calls the decorations 'their pleasures' and specifies the colours she would use for their restoration. There are hundreds of sample patches in her drawing books, of shades of pale blue to compare with the inlaid stones that presumably the craftsmen were to use when redoing the patterns and leaves embedded in the white marble. There are sketches and paintings of churches and temples, mausoleums, mosques, palaces and pavilions. Yes, I'll see them one day. And no I won't sell them to Sotheby's. Sufi will invent a thousand rhymes about holly and folly and bells, snow, Santa, reindeer, cheer, etc. He says the trick is to introduce things not normally associated with Christmas and he is going to get together with other poets and picket KeyNotes's card factory to increase the fee from £2 a couplet to £5. He will yet, he says, be acknowledged as the Robespierre, or at least the Arthur Scargill, of the Christmas-card-jingle-wallas.

'My Sexy Santa was a winner!
A rhyme should at least pay for dinner?'

I shout up the stairs.

'I nearly forgot with all this Sally business. The Brighton Literary festival called.'

That brings him down like a cat off a hot lead roof.

'Yes?' Sufi is eager.

'They wanted to know if you, as a local Indian writer, would chair the session at which Tarun Bahadur has been invited to speak,' I say.

'The arsehole patronizes me,' he says. 'They've invited him to speak?'

'Well he is a Booker Prize winner. Anyway, I know how you feel and I said you wouldn't because you can't get past the first five pages of any of his books. OK?'

Sufi knows me too well.

'Did they leave a phone number? Where's their phone number? It doesn't matter if it doesn't pay. To appear on the platform with Tarun ... You didn't really fucking say that, did you?' He is not sure. Hee hee.

'Of course I didn't. I said you'd call back and check your diary and would be glad to be asked.'

Sufi actually kisses me on the cheek. He must be sneaking off to anti-aversion therapy classes when I'm not looking.

Oh, he sucked up to them. I heard him call back. Glad to be asked. Oh yes, yes, he knew Tarun's CV by heart.

He isn't ashamed of my overhearing that sort of thing any more. Like he used to shut the door when he went to the lavatory for so many years. And now when he's grown flabby and really should care, he sits on the loo reading old copies of *Private Eye* and laughing out loud, unconcerned as to what sounds I hear from whichever end of him. Sufi, Sufi, why do I love you? Still?

Yes, now I know that you're something of a poet and something of a fraud. I now know why. I have heard over and over again what your father told you, that poetry was for layabouts and loafers, for the amusement of parasites, drunkards and drug-addicts. It was the profession of confidence tricksters who had to sell words. Like selling fresh air. In some recess of your mind you believed it.

Engineering was real work. You came to England to be an engineer, didn't you? And ran away and joined the Arts Laboratory in London and grew your hair and started writing and singing songs. And then you discovered you were a poet and that people took poetry-reading seriously. Especially if the poets pretended that all they cared about was beer and money and bitching about each other at the Poetry Society in

Earls Court from where we'd stumble at midnight to go on to someone's dingy room till dawn. Oh Sufi, I remember those days, catching the early-morning trains, tanked-up on Special Brew and Barley Wine and god knows what other poisons, and sleeping curled-up into you and waking to stroke your long shoulder-length black hair. The hangovers! You wouldn't listen to me and graduate to wine and you made me ashamed of the fact that my family had brought me up, unselfconsciously knowing the difference between one vintage and the other, one grape and the next and one growing region of the world and the other. One wasn't allowed to mention that amongst poets. Poets knew red from white and that was all and that was what street-respectability demanded. Anything further would be foppish, snobbish, selling out to the bourgeoisie, the enemies of the written word.

'So you've changed your mind about TB's talent, have you? Sounded like it from the fawning phone call.'

'You wouldn't know what a fawn is. Anyway, it was the afternoon of the Faun. What did you want me to do, say that his novels are shit and back out?'

'No, but you needn't have said, "Sure, his inventiveness has set a new benchmark in the imaginative grammar." Bit thick, don't we think?'

'We can think what we like. What we say must offer concessions to reality. The reality is they offered me fifty pounds. You don't want me to do it now, but when you get a bad mood you'll start on about how I don't work, and how you work the skin off your knuckles to keep me and crap like that. It was my house you know, in London, which you put on the market without telling me. I came home and found a board outside my own home. I had to live behind a board which said "For Sale". How could I call literary friends there?'

'You didn't have any literary friends. You'd fought with them all. In fact, you didn't have any friends.'

'I knew Mr Patel at the corner. We used to talk.'

'And you agreed we had to move because the creditors were calling and the bailiffs and god knows who. Fifty pounds is lovely darling, but you'll have to read his books.'

'Or a review or two and then pretend.'

'This whisky is piss,' I said. 'After thirty years you don't know that I don't want water with it?'

Jo picks up the bottle of scotch and looks at it. There's very little left. She clicks her teeth. There's something she's not saying.

'Patrick's party last night. They must have run out and come upstairs and raided your whisky and then put water in it when they panicked.'

'The bastards. Adultery,' I said.

'They could have asked instead of this childish attempt at subterfuge.'

'The seventh sin. You know Jo, I went to an Anglican school and we had this brute from England coming down from the Mission every year and we had to endure a week of his preaching for an hour a day. He had little felt animals and figures and pieces of landscape, felt trees and felt grass, which he put on a felt board mounted on an easel and the animals stuck, and sitting in the auditorium we all thought it was the power of the Christian God. All us Sikhs and Muslims and Hindus and Parsees.'

I had never told her any of this before.

'Is your school still there?'

'Very much so.'

'That's where I want you to take me. To show me where you grew up.'

'You trying to distract me, aren't you, from the adultery.'

'From what?'

'I told you. There was this one missionary called Reverend Mullins and he told us about God giving Moses Nine Commandments. He stuck the felt mountain to his felt board and then he stuck on a felt Moses as he told the story and then the felt burning bush and the felt tablets. And the tablets had Nine Commandments. Some innocent amongst us protested and said that his mum had told him there were Ten Commandments, but Reverend Mullins wouldn't budge. He had the boy brought out after assembly and flogged. The next day at the religious assembly there was a riot. Five or ten Christian boys had brought their bibles in and consulted their fathers and priests. The word had spread in school that the Seventh Commandment, which the Reverend Mullins had conveniently omitted, was the pornographic one, to do with doing it to a woman other than your wife, the one whose discussion by a figure of authority would give us great pleasure. When several boys raised their hands and their objections, Reverend Mullins conceded.

'I'll give you the Seventh Commandment,' he said. 'It is thou shalt not commit adultery.'

'And what's that?' we all shouted to make him say the dirty thing.

'It's when milkmen pour water in their milk and sell it to you. Now none of you are from milkmen's families so there is no danger that you will ever sell milk or commit adultery.'

⟨◎⟩

The bastards didn't tell me that the fifty pounds included putting up ten posters in public places. My name is on them in small print and Bahadur's presence announced in bold. Fuck it. I've got nothing to do.

And so as I'm doing it, I hear the sound of rapping from the lecture hall down the corridor. This college is deserted. It's the holidays. But of course there are the summer schools and the students from abroad on their summer course. The one I should have been lecturing at.

'Let us today look at the conceits of Donne who wants to talk about sex but does it through describing the mingling of his blood with that of his mistress through a flea which has fed on them both. Any takers? I see many hands. Will that Japanese young lady please put away her camera. It distracts me from Donne. And get her kit off which will distract me even further from Donne. Tee hee. Tee hee.'

I pin the poster on the crowded board, discarding five or six useless, purposeless notices for Yoga and computing tuition and the like to make space and frame this great literary event with a border of space. Then I look in on the lecture through the window.

It is young William trying to recite something to music and lo and behold, no one is listening. Yes, he has a class full of young people, and some not so young, with books on their desks and pens poised to receive and all they are getting is rap. And I look at William and he knows it. But he is on the rack and has not time to stand and stare back. I have, oh idle hour! And I catch the eye of a girl in the front row. She looks as patient as a motorist on a B road stuck behind agricultural machinery, with no space to overtake. In her hands she has a book which she is reading, without bothering to disguise this fact from William who is supposed to be holding her undivided etc. She glances back at me and shuts the book. Oh yes, I know the cover. *The Penguin Metaphysicals.* Her glance towards me is not focussed – a face at the window, perhaps the Pakistani college cleaner looking in to see if the wretched class is over so he can do some work. She is bored.

Serves the bastards right. I walk past the second window. There they all are, the daisies of this spring's poetic crop, the Japanese, the swarthy Spanish, the mischievous Italian boys and the Americans. You can spot the Americans by their mass produced clothes.

At least they are not talking amongst themselves. My heart goes out to William. He reads on and his voice wanders. His poem doesn't have the cadence of speech. It is all forced rhyming couplets and bragging sentences culled from the dismissive argot of today's brain-dead youth.

Fie.

'Our century,' says TB, and then he laughs. 'I mean the last one really, the twentieth, but I keep forgetting, is filled with writers in exile and writings about exile. Its genius is in Henry James, Conrad, Nabokov, Joyce, Solzhenitsyn, who was not even allowed to physically realize that exile, V.S.Naipaul and others you may add. It speaks of the homeless condition. That's what I feel, as a writer, I have inherited. No heartland, no home.'

He waits for the words to have effect. Sufi sits next to him at the table on the platform. The audience is transfixed. It has been a rich reading and Sufi has behaved himself and now he takes a sip of water and I can see from his face that he is going to turn. Judgement has come and mercy has gone as the reggae singers used to say.

'I thought you owned this big house in Netting Hill,' he says.

TB can parry that.

'I mean metaphorically homeless,' he says to his chairperson. This audience doesn't know how to react.

'Metaphorically in exile?'

'Yeah,' says TB, nodding and biting his lip.

'With a few million in the bank and the advance you got for your next book and two abandoned ex-wives to support, I'd like a bit of this metaphorical exile myself.'

The audience now laughs.

'You are being frivolous, Sufi. Pain and nostalgia go beyond and deeper than anything that money or the entanglements of life can heal.'

'What about the pain and exile of Kurds or Tamils fed up with the war in Sri Lanka or the Africans who are set adrift in rotten boats trying to get to Europe? That's real exile. Money, one-thousandth of what you've got, would solve a bit of their pain.'

'I am sure,' says TB, picking up the three paperbacks of his oeuvre he'd brought to read from. 'You should go into charity work. Feed the hungry, clothe the naked. I thought we were here to discuss literature.'

And he gets up and leaves and all Sufi can do is to start clapping and pretend this was a planned exit.

At the reception afterwards, where the Festival serves red and white wine, the groupies gather round TB and I spot Sufi alone drinking two glasses of wine in quick succession off a tray. No one talks to him. I don't want to walk up to him and say he was quite right. He knows I am here, I think.

A guy approaches Sufi, a white guy with Rasta locks and blue penetrating eyes.

I have to leave. Sally is packing to go to her parents' for the holidays and she says a friend is to come round and I must look her over to see if I will let her use Sally's room for a few days. And then I'm away to London myself to see my younger sister on stage in the West End. She is in *Major Barbara*. Oh, she's not playing the lead or anything and I am back on the last train. Poor Sufi. I think he earned his fifty quid.

There she is again, the literary groupie, the harpie of boredom, the girl from the front row of the summer school class – William's class. And she is walking towards me. But no, not towards me. Three yards away to shamelessly accost the waiter with the white wine and take two off him. She offers the other glass to black beauty, a fellow student with dark lips and hair so straight and shiny it looks like a wig, or purple with allure. I sip my wine and thirst away.

'I took the course to meet real writers. William's whole outlook is post-modern which means he is beyond his time.'

'Beyond his and wastin' mine,' says the black girl with a lilt in her voice.

'I came from Jamaica to get away from all this bullshit and the English them, they throw it back in my face.'

So I leave. I walk deliberately past the golden girl, the one I have called the princess of boredom in my head and try and exchange glances, but one can't swop old lamps for new outside the pantomime and she must see that my flames are near snuffing.

Someone follows me out of the tent. Some bore is going to stop me and berate me for being rude to the great TB.

William says, 'Can I have a word? You remember me?'

'Words, words, words. Mostly lies. Didn't you hear the great novelist? Bastard. Lying bastard.'

'I agreed with you,' says the boy.

'So you can have a word. Have a million. They never got me nowhere, man.'

'I need help.'

'Sorry man, I've got no cash. But have a heart. You got the job.'

'No, no. I am not after money. Listen, Mr Akhtar, I can give you some money.'

'I don't want your dirty money, earned by talking rubbish.'

'They made a mistake. The interview panel. They should have appointed you.'

'And why?'

'Because these students who come to this course want real poetry lectures and shit, and I'm fucked, Mr Akhtar, I don't know crap about your kinda poetry. Real poetry.'

'So now it's being belittled as 'real poetry' is it?'

'They've all seen *Shakespeare in Love* and that, and they want what you got. They told me. They are complaining to the dean. They want Metaphoricals ...'

'Metaphysicals,' I say. 'Yeah, whatever,' he says.

'Don't use that word "whatever". It implies that you are bored and those who have nothing to say have no right to be bored. They have a reason to be, of course. But you get my drift. Don't use the word in my presence to cut me off.'

'I'll do whatever you say, Mr. Akhtar. Stop using, start using, just like you want—if you'll help me. How to say this, Mr Akhtar, I feel kinda ashamed, you know. Please man, you gotta help me. I can't resign now. They won't let me. The college says carry on and if the students don't like it they can leave, but they are all like rebelling and will go on strike. I don't get to sleep man. I've taken the wrong turning and like the dream has turned into a nightmare. I can't get out of bed in the mornings and face that class. See, what I know they don't want.'

'So what am I expected to do?'

'Help me. Tell me what to do.'

'Me tell you? You got the job man, I got a kick in the arse from little kids. Eminem or somebody. OK, William, that's your name isn't it? You won and now you're making out you've lost. Forget the students. Say your thing, talk to the air, disturb the ether and laugh all the way to the bank. Balls to the students and what they want!'

'Balls?' he asks.

'You heard me. Big balls.'

'No man,' he says, crestfallen. 'So you won't help me out, man?'

'Oh, OK, I will,' I say. 'I'll put you on track.'

'I'll give you half my salary, man.'

'Look, don't be vulgar,' I say and start to walk away. This tent, in which TB is still glorying in the adulation of people who can't read, has begun to leak pseuds. Must away. No doubt the Arts wallahs will send the fifty quid on. Or maybe they were there and will fine me for being frank and just send thirty quid or something. The rules may have changed. Bastards.

'I didn't mean it badly, Mr Akhtar,' says young William. 'I know you don't need the money, but I don't know how else to ask.'

'You are mistaken on so many counts, I feel sorry for you,' I say. 'Come on.'

I take young William home and we climb the stairs to my room in the attic and I fetch a bottle of Sainsbury's Claret and two glasses from the kitchen. The house is deserted. Joanna has gone to London for the night to see her sister, who can't act for toffee, make a fool of herself with her plum accent on the London stage. The conceit of the well-born whiteys. Not the same as the conceits of Donne.

'I tell you what. Easy-peasy. Just get on with it. Choose a theme: love, fame, betrayal, loss. Take loss. Get some lines out, read them. Shakespeare on Loss, something simple. The lament from Mark Antony. His mate's been murdered. Tell them what that's about. Then the Lucy poems from Wordsworth – his girl's dead. Then to Yeats:

> 'Does the imagination dwell the most
> Upon the woman won or the woman lost?
> If on the lost, admit you turned aside
> From the labyrinth of another's being out of pride
> Or some silly over-subtle thought,
> And if memory recur, the sun's under eclipse
> And the day blotted out.'

'Wow, that's heavy,' says William and he grabs my arm. 'I have to take all this down.'

'Don't bother.'

I will take William in hand. A devil wells up inside me – I can see him just under my nose, the emergent genie of spite who is enjoying subduing this winner of interviews, watching him crawl and ask cap-in-hand for help. Yes, I shall help him as the hand of the puppeteer helps its glove puppet.

'I am going to write you a lecture,' I say, sitting at the computer on the funny chair that Joanna has bought me, in the hope that it will preserve my spine. My spine, I tell her, is pickled in fat and nothing can touch it. It is like an eel in a thick jelly, I can feel it. But she says she sometimes doubts the existence of my spine.

The boy pulls up a chair from the other side of the bed.

'A lecture?'

'Yes, you can read, can't you? Or do you just have to shoot six-guns to qualify as a gangster rapping poetwalla?'

'Oh yes, I can read, Mr Akhtar,' the fool says. He can't even spot a joke. All irony is lost. The man has the gift of turning gold to lead.

You start by saying, 'Today we consider poems of Loss.' You've grabbed their attention. Then you talk about loss, the personal dimension. The loss through death, the breaking up of a friendship, the end of love. Get it? Then you go straight into Tennyson. Just read it aloud and let them wonder. Let it mount and fuck their brains:

'Behold we know not anything
I can but trust that good shall fall
At last – far off – at last to all
And every winter change to spring.'

'Hey man that's too much,' says William.

'Not quite, there's more,' I say and begin to type and he looks over my shoulder. I pronounce it as I type.

'So runs my dream, but what am I?
An infant crying in the night
An infant crying for the light;
And with no language but a cry ...'

'Then what do I do?' he asks.

'By this time they'll be swooning. You'll have to get on your mobile and call the fire brigade or the cops to stop them attacking you and tearing off your clothes.'

'Yeah,' he says. Our William is low on the exaggerated oblique.

I write the rest of the lecture for him with all the stage directions thrown in and we finish another bottle of the same wine and then I print the lecture out and by five in the morning he's revised it and read it aloud and he's ready for noon the next day. So he goes off to get some sleep clutching the papers.

Joanna comes back.

'Anything?'

'Nothing. How was Sarah Bernhardt?'

'She was fine. She's understudying a bigger role.'

'*I need a little sugar in my bowl, I need a little hot dog in my roll,*' I sing.

Joanna isn't in the mood.

William comes back at three, full of it.

They lapped it up.

Joanna doesn't know what 'it' is and who has lapped what up. Was I selling drugs now? But I say it is business and take him up to my study. God knows she must think we're having a homosexual go in the middle of the afternoon because she knocks on the door and asks if we want tea. Joanna is not a tea dispenser. The kids have hell getting her to make breakfast.

'Smash hit. Lotus, the American girl. You met her, sir. Or she was next to you in the tent, you know talking to the black girl. She is called Lotus and I ... I started by saying I've rethought the whole thing and gone back to the old ways – I said I am going to listen to their demands and then I started as you said and I ... I read it through. Quite well, I think. She loved it. I mean they all did.'

'Ah, did she? Well your next lecture is on memory and desire. Turn her on.'

'Yeah, but what do I say?'

'I'll type it up. Done, like a hot-crossed bun.'

I get on the computer. Joanna comes in with the tea looking for signs of unbuttoned or hastily buttoned trousers. I do intros, saying that William is interested in memory and desire and Joanna is a veteran.

She leaves and I kick the computer. Memory and desire, stirring dull roots with spring rain. So what did T.S. Eliot mean? The lecture is ready for delivery by six that evening. We are shortening the spans. William puts in an order for seven more and I say I can get working on them while he is not in the room and then he can just take them and learn them and deliver them.

'Mr Akhtar, I need to.'

I know he wants to give me some money so I growl at him.

'Don't insult me or I'll kick you downstairs and trample on your heart.'

We decide to meet on the beach the next day. William comes running across the sand.

'Brighton,' I say. 'Fish and chips and adultery.' He looks at me, the notes of the lecture still in his hands. He is almost trembling with success.

'Not me, John Osborne said that.'

'Who's John Osborne? Shall I take it down?'

'Of no consequence. How did it go?'

'She loved it!'

'She?'

'The class, all of them. But I was talking about Lotus, you know, the girl who sits in the front row.'

'The girl from Dirty Dick, Arkansas, sure. Why did she like it?' Of course I knew which girl he was talking about.

'She said it was exactly what she had felt but was never able to say. That's it. That's what she said and she begged for the next one and what's it going to be, man?'

'It is going to be far reaching. What's this girl like?'

'Like? She's like ... lemme see – Latin complexion, black hair, leggy.'

'Eyes?'

'Good.'

'I didn't ask about her vision. Eyes, man, her eyes. Are they big, sparkling, jewelled ...'

'That's it. Jewelled, but sad.'

'So go for her. The next one has to be the greatest chat-up line known to civilization. You've got to hook her and wrestle her and tire her and pull her in. So the next lecture is on seduction. The lines used to do just that. From Shakespeare to your Bob Dylan who abuses to seduce.'

We go home and work on that one and when we've got it done, it's the perfect vehicle.

'So you're set for the big conquest.'

'No, no, no,' he says. 'The dean told me when they called me to sign, that that's not what they wanted here. They've had too many sexual harassment accusations, which the uni has had to shell out for. So no contact or out, finished. Zero tolerance.'

'OK, I get it. You want to hit on her but you're scared, so bring her to dinner here. That's surely allowed? Say you're taking her to see a real poet. Joanna would be delighted. I'll give you one of my books to prove that you're not bullshitting – published in India, but it's the only one I've got.

◎

She's gorgeous. Joanna is mightily intrigued and the boy William is a fumbler and a fool. Joanna watches me watching Lotus.

'What an unusual name,' says Joanna. 'How did it come about?'

'My parents,' says Lotus.

That figures, I think. One's parents usually give one a name ... and then. And then, not as dumb as one may have thought.

'... my parents didn't name me after the flower, they named me after the yoga position. It was a joke between them.'

'I see. Some people call their kids Brooklyn because that's where the kid was conceived.'

'I think that's the idea, Mr Akhtar,' she says, getting all shy. 'There's still some little secret between them – about me being conceived with one of them in the lotus position? Though I've never quite figured out how that works, because it's squatting cross-legged.'

'It seems difficult. But like camels going through the eyes of needles, with the *Kama Sutra* all things are possible.'

'I guess,' she says. 'And I kinda like it because it's poetic like the flower.'

'It's a pity your name isn't Budd, like Billy Budd in the story, then you'd be called Lotus Budd. Lotus buds are very pretty, so it would suit you.'

She blushes and Joanna raises her eyebrows.

'Or you could be called Lotus Eater. Like if your surname was Eater,' says Willie. He is greeted by the silence this deserves. No, Lotus is not going for him in a big way.

'Are you enjoying Brighton?' Joanna asks. 'It must be a change after New York.'

'The change is the lectures and William. Gosh, when I got here and William played that cheesy trick of doing Rap and stuff in his first lecture, it was like I'd stepped back into the Bronx and I'd come all the way to like "learn something"?' Her habit of adopting a tone for quotation marks was going to get annoying.

'I don't understand. He did what?' asked Joanna.

'Oh it doesn't matter now. That's all memory. And now I love it, Brighton.'

'And it's down to William's brilliance? Give us a sample of the brilliance, William,' demands Joanna playfully.

'He's a professional, Jo, you'll have to join his classes,' I say, scrambling to cover for him.

'That's right and welcome too,' says little Willie.

'I can't wait that long,' says Joanna. 'Tell me what he does that's special.'

'He makes you understand, or the poetry he brings us does: the difference between the lover dying and the lover living forever and it still being the same thing because the poet has immortalized her?'

'Sounds good,' says Jo.

'Shakespeare,' I say.

'Ah!' says Lotus. 'We asked him who the writer was but William wouldn't say.'

Shit! I had only written the number of the sonnet and hadn't added 'By William Shakespeare' in brackets and that must have left little Willie floundering in front of the class.

'He teases you,' I say.

'It's my lecturing technique,' says Willie.

'But Shakespeare must have been the gangster rapper of his day,' says Joanna. 'He was quite flash and gorgeous anyway.'

'He was nothing of the sort. He was a stingy two-bit actor whose mind was the greatest poetry machine ever – it's how he saw the contours of personality, places, moods, reality, all in texture,' says the girl, probably recalling some lecture.

'Yes, but he looked gorgeous. I've seen him in the movies,' says Willie.

'They always choose the wrong actor. Shakespeare should be old and with a pot belly and ugly, then we can separate appreciation from celebrity swooning,' Lotus adds.

'And if he were revealed as ugly, old, stingy and smelly?' asks Jo.

'Who cares? The poetry's the thing,'

'That's noble,' says Jo.

'No, it's selfish. Think of the wasted lives that don't discover how to look at everything in flashes of lightning. Cushy jobs, unloved wives. When I was a kid in Virginia, I used to go down to the graveyards and look at the tombstones, a hundred, two hundred years. They had beautiful rhymes, some of them. All about the life gone by undiscovered.'

'Lotus's Elegy in a Country Churchyard,' I say.

'Come again?'

'It's a poem. Very beautiful. Willie knows it,' I reply.

That was wicked. Willie sputters. He looks at me as though I have kicked him in the balls, not wanting revenge but an explanation for the hurt.

'Go on then, recite a bit of it,' Lotus says to Willie. 'When he gets down to it, his voice is music.'

'Not going to bore everyone,' says Willie. 'With graveyards and death while we are eating.'

'It's not about death, is it?' asks Lotus, all fluttering innocence. And now I see what she's playing at. Of course she knows the poem. They must read it in Virginia or the Bronx or wherever it is they impregnate each other in the lotus position. She is playing with Willie.

'Just two lines, so that Joanna can get the rich tenor,' she says.

Willie darts a look at me. A drowning man.

'Aw, he's shy,' I say. 'Let's do it together, William.'

'Come under the shadow of this red rock and I will show you fear in a handful of dust.'

Willie is relieved. 'I will show you, fear in a handful of dust,' he says theatrically.

I smile at Lotus. Jo to the rescue.

'Quite enough poetry,' she says. 'William is right to save it for the right time and right place.'

'Can't wait,' says the lady of the lake, my lily, my Lotus.

After they go that night the snow comes down and Joanna starts an argument about the guttering being jammed and the walls of the house coming down.

'I can't climb three stories onto the roof. I've got astrophobia,' I protest.

'It's agrophobia.'

'I mean fear of astrology. It was predicted that my death would involve heights and gutters and a dying fall.'

After years of having being fended off, Jo knows better than to try and get me to do this job. She lies awake fretting about the snow, bitter and jealous and using her worry like a cross.

'Unappreciated Beings,' I say to Willie when he comes for the last dose, the final lecture.

'What's that?'

'That's your last lecture. On the neglected creatures of this world. The tragedy of wasted lives. Toasters who've burnt their toast, rappers who can't beat the rap, plumbers whose depths haven't been plumbed ... you could go on.'

'Sounds untold, man,' says Willie in his wisdom.

'I've sketched it out,' I say. I'd worked on it for a night and day ever since the dinner, ever since I couldn't put Lotus and her legs and the wonders between them out of my mind.

Willie is suddenly embarrassed. He pulls out eight fifty-pound notes and puts them on the table next to the computer.

'I had to spend the rest to live,' he says.

I take the notes and tuck them back in his trouser pocket.

'Don't do that again, or I'll tear the lecture up,' I say.

Then it occurs to me.

'How good are you with gutters?'

'Gutters?' once more he is lost.

'Not as in "lying in". That's my department. Cleaning out, climbing up ladders.'

So it is done. Willie cleans out Jo's gutters and mutters the verses he later utters. Sheesh-kebab! Talk about poetry, man. That's pure rap! See?

Unappreciated beings:

'Full many a gem of purest ray serene.

The dark unfathom'd caves of ocean bear ...'

Willie hands Joanna the book as he works. She tests him on the verse which he repeats over and over. She starts looking through the text. Then he leaves to get cleaned up for the lecture and straight after the lecture he is going to ask Lotus out.

'Make it a place of magic and mystery.'

'I'll ask her to the pictures,' he says imaginatively.

'Yes, you do that. Then you can fumble in the dark.'

He phones to say he'll be late home from the office. 'You don't have an office,' I say.

'Don't be pedantic,' he says. Then he tells me.

He's met a long-lost friend, just wandering about the Brighton antique shops and, as though to sweeten the lie, he says there might be some cash in it, because he's going to remind the friend of a long-lost loan, because he looks flush now that he's moved from poetry to fake furniture.

(◎)

It was misty and I waited in the churchyard. Good rhymes:

> *Here lies Mary Benn*
> *Taken from us when*
> *The Great Death walked.*
> *It will return,*
> *But she'll come no more again.*

How my heart leapt when I got that note. A daredevil. She hadn't bothered to seal it. It was in an open envelope, slipped through the letter box . The envelope said 'Sufi'.

And the note was elegant. Or was it? I read it ten times over.

Dear Sufi,
I've been, on my perambulations around Sussex, looking at churchyards. How morbid is that! I would love to meet you on your own in my favourite one, good on epitaphs, spooky and sobering and oddly renewing. It's St. Alphages on Boar Lane. You turn left off the road outside Great Wattenden. Will you see me there Thursday evening? School will be out. I must move on and have spied pastures new. It gets dark by five; so can

you make it four? Then there's a village pub with delicious food. Perhaps you know it. But perhaps I've overstepped and you won't be there.
Your Lotus.

My Lotus? Would I not be there? Were the metaphorical wild horses to take flesh and be hired by Joanna as a team with their harnesser and handler for Thursday ...

Her car stops in the white of the fog.

She looks around. I am early, of course, and won't reveal myself yet. She takes it for granted that I haven't arrived and walks from stone to stone leaning over them to read.

I tiptoe up behind her. Could there have been a mistake, a metaphysical trick which sent the wrong note in the wrong envelope? No. She knew. What had she said about Shakespeare being ugly and old and even smelly and acceptable? Of course she was talking to him.

Christ have mercy on Lizzie Liszt
Never married, often kissed.
Women would she were in hell
It's by us men that she'll be missed

'So simple isn't it? The rhyme and the life,' I say, startling her.

She turns her head, a swan. She is wearing a brown embroidered coat whose collar rises to her neck.

'Yes, I knew you'd understand,' she says, standing up. 'Thank you for turning up. For not thinking I am a silly girl.'

Heart, O troubled heart – sit down, shut up!

'You, you're the one who's seen through the game.'

'It wasn't difficult, was it? Poor Willie. I suppose most of the others were fooled when he said he'd go back to the old ways now that we demanded them, but I've been an actress and I can tell when someone is reading someone else's lines.'

She had an angelic smile, twisted like the bow of Cupid at the corners – and how silly is that? As she would say.

'He's very useful,' I said.

'I know. He told me he had been asked by Joanna to do her guttering and I could feel the hand of Sufi on the tiller. Thursday from lunchtime. Keep them both busy.'

'Yeah,' I said and she caught my shirt collar and brought her face right up to mine.

William is perched on the roof and I've convinced him to tie a rope round his waist but I don't know where to secure the other end so I've tied it to a door knob. I thought of the leg of a bed in Sufi's attic, but it's a single bed and if he fell, his weight might drag the bed right across to the window.

Is he glad the course is over now?

Relieved.

Is he going back to writing rap poetry and doing recordings?

He is going to finish this roof first, but it needs a new kind of filling, a thing he's heard of on telly that will stop all leaks and sliding tiles. It will only take him today and maybe tomorrow.

So I fetch the Thompson's blue directory and find him the roofing supplies pages and read the addresses. He comes down from the roof.

There's a lot of nailing to be done so he'd better catch the shops before they shut.

He asks for a map of the district, an A to Z of Brighton and environs. Do I have one? Lotus has taken his car and his map is in it.

'I've got a local book,' I say.

I go and look in my bedroom. It isn't there.

But after he goes, I find it. On the attic bed and there's a ruler in a page with a circle around Great Wattenden. So a hunting we will go. We'll catch a fox and put him in a box. O Sufi!

◎

Then another car drives up. Don't I know that sound? Jo's little Citroen. She steps out and she looks at the two of us in the mist. She doesn't say anything. She is a silhouette but I know it's her, without a coat. She has spotted us. I grab Lotus's hand and try and retreat into the mist.

'Don't worry,' is what Joanna says before she gets into her car and is gone. There's nothing *she* can object to, except that I lied.

◎

As though I wouldn't know what was going on? As though I can't tell every fleck of intonation, from every vowel sound in his so called jocular fob-offs, that they conceal lies and the stench of lies. Face me? He couldn't tell me those lies looking in my eyes.

Adultery is what adults do, but Sufi is no more than a stupid little boy. Fiction is deceit, he says, yeah yeah yeah, but lies are just lies. The bastard, the bitch and the fool. He thinks I didn't catch on and the last penny dropped when the poor boy was trying to memorize Thomas Gray. As though he would – fifty pages in a day. And I shouldn't blame him because he did do the guttering for free and even bought the bits and hired the ladder which he said he'd borrowed, but it has the hire-firm's name on the side, the idiot.

So he must owe Sufi, I calculated. Thomas Gray. Graveyard romance. Give me a break as they would say. I may be very foolish, but don't play me for a fool.

Out, out, damned Sufi, out I say. Ohhhhh, not for that American Bimbo. Poetry. My constipated arse! Poetry? She? The bimbo of Broadway, the broad of Bimbistan, conceived when her mother's legs were twisted in a lotus position, oh yes, a great invitation to imagination, wasn't it? When I'd cooked fish pie. Little madam didn't think I knew what she was doing but I clocked her, the whore. Trying to make him think of limbs and holes and hers. The whippet, sitting and eating my dinner – his wife's dinner.

And what's completely ridiculous is that at his age he's playing Cyrano de Bergerac. The deluded, deluded bastard with his paunch and the spare tyre hanging off his tired flesh and the cliche of the black student in the basement and getting an erection off of his and his girlfriends' doings and noises. Sick

sick sick. None of you are going to be milkmen so it doesn't apply to you.

It's two o'clock and I am damned if I'm going to bed. His stuff is in the hallway and here he comes.

'No need to tiptoe, Cyrano, I am awake.'

'Oh what a dinner. She'd called all her friends to meet a real poet and the kids quarrelled over quotes and I had to patch it up.'

I can't believe this, he's playing the 'nothing has happened' card.

'Get the fuck out of this house. No, don't sit down. Get out now.'

'What's come over you?'

'You think you can play me for a fool?'

'I wasn't thinking I could play you for anything.'

And that hurt. Yes, he was telling the truth. He hadn't even considered me. Not a fool, not anything, not there!

'But you behaved as though I was gullible and gulled and wouldn't realize that you had turned into a milkman and were watering the product. I saw you with that bitch. "Can you recite some more poems, Mr Akhtar?"'

I shouldn't have tried her American accent.

'Your baggage is in the hall,' I said.

'Just like at the airports. Baggage in hall,' he said and started putting on his shoes.

Then I didn't want him to go. I wanted him to stay and quarrel all night. I wanted to drag the guilt out of him, to shout and scream at him and accuse him and remember the abortion in May 1972 and the way I bled and how he had to go to a bloody poetry reading because it was important and 'the boys from Faber' would be there. Faber and Faber, the poet-adulterer's excuse.

But he was going, and suddenly as he left I knew where he was going. He was going to the bimbo. It hadn't occurred to me. I had seen him in my mind's eye wandering, repentantly, to Brighton station and then I'd drive alongside and pick him up and all would be forgiven. But now he was determined to get the hell out and do the Seventh Sin, the Big A. I wasn't going to let him. He hadn't already, but my casting him out would force him to it. Adultery is what adults do and she, just a child, a stupid American child with conceits about poetry.

It was I who had in the flesh suffered for poetry. I had gone hungry because my husband was a poet. I smiled as I caught myself thinking this. Ridiculous. My feet rushed to the front door and I barred it without thinking, without pride.

And then a flush of dignity came back. Free agents. We had married as free agents. Not the anger, that's not what came back, just a restraining dignity, just a thought and a rush of blood to the head. A thought about the balance of power. If I barred the door to his departure now, I would be giving away too much. I pretended I had come to look for his scarf from the hat stand and I gave it to him and cursed him again as he left. That way he'd remember me as proud and unyielding, not as a pathetic beggar, as he walked down the street to ... I put it out of mind. He could go where he liked. If I barred his way now, he would crow about his triumph for weeks. Not vocally, just smirking as he lies with his useless, unpoetic bulk around the house and stinks it out with his rotting intestines. He has nothing else to do. The epic is not progressing.

She is fucking welcome to him. Or maybe, just welcome, not fucking welcome. Could I care less?

Yes.

I am standing outside her window. And she's got *West Side Story* on the CD player and she dances. I dare not go in. I don't know the first thing about her. Does she share this room in the student's hostel with another girl perhaps?

'I feel pretty,
Oh so pretty,
I feel pretty and witty and gay ...'

She dances, or perhaps that's the silhouette of her moving about the room in some other sort of trance and then I get it. She has returned to Willie. My gods, he is the roommate. Am I falling into a trap myself? Has my whole judgement of people and what they do and why they do gone 'phut'?

Willie opens the door, not at all surprised to see me.

'I don't want to stand in your way, man, but I'm just telling her you are not interested. She's too immature for you ...'

'What's the bag for?' she asks, not getting out of the chair, her legs drawn up on it, oriental style.

Thespian, dramatize thyself.

'Joanna's thrown me out.'

Willie puts his hands on his ears and goes to the kitchen of his two-room furnished flat, to get me some of the coffee they are drinking, and he says, 'I could see it coming: your wife doesn't understand you.'

'Not true. She understands me too well.'

'There's so much there to understand. I've told Willie all about us,' Lotus says. She tries to switch her limbs into something resembling that lotus position that allows a man to impregnate a woman. willie has put on Dvorak, very low on his silver-and-blue CD player.

'I thought you didn't like real music,' I say as he hands me the coffee. And I am looking for the opening in the lotus.

'I bought three CDs which the Classical Department sales jock in HMV said I could start with. Beethoven's *Fifth Symphony*, Rachmaninov's *Piano Concerto* and this one, *New Worlds*.'

'World. Just one,' says Lotus. 'But when does she want you back?'

'Never.'

'So what do you want?'

I wasn't expecting that sort of question.

'I'm looking for the angel. You see, when I was born, a Sufi saint told my mum that I'd spot an angel, a real live one. That I would recognize her and she would be my light and my salvation. That's why they called me Sufi.'

'Would the angel know she was one?'

'Not necessarily, so it makes it harder.'

I sat down.

'Why are we beating round the bush? Before you walked in, she was screaming at me, because I said you wouldn't tolerate her. So now it's fixed, man. She wants you, you want her, why don't you guys fuck off and leave me alone to get some sleep.'

'It's not that easy, is it?' Lotus asks.

'I don't think it is.' I said

'Sufi, I told Willie. I don't understand what you're doing in a place like Brighton. If you wrote those lectures, Sufi, you should be at a university, at Oxford or some place. And your work, the epic you told us about, I'd love to read it and when you said no one wants to even look at it and that ... that your wife has stopped even bothering about the pages you've added ... that just made me cry. If it was me I'd stay awake till you finished on the computer and then sneak a look at the lines, man. They are bound to be gold. Your stuff, the one from the Delhi publisher, it's very powerful. Willie showed me the book, I've got it ... '

'Maybe I'll take a train to London in the morning.'

'And what'll you do there?'

'I'll hole up somewhere and finish the poem. The large work, ambition beyond ability perhaps. To write about the Indian and the British romance, tragedy, comedy. About how the ruled corrupt the rulers.'

We walk to her house in the dawn and I take her hand. She is going to go with me to London.

Keats's house. Couldn't get away from the area. Phoned Faqr (yes, it *is* pronounced like that and he refuses to change it and that gets him a huge amount of attention which he otherwise doesn't merit) to ask him if he had a spare room. After all he is one guy, gay as a bunting, living in this large house, five floors and eight bedrooms, all on his own, except for the occasional boyfriends to whom he plays Simon and Garfunkel so loudly that you can hear it to the end of the road where our flat used to be.

'Faqr's had joy,' Joanna would say of a Sunday morning when we heard *The Only Living Boy in New York* floating across the back fences and gardens of West Hampstead.

'I can't do you, boyo,' Faqr says. He thinks he can pass for a Welshman.

'A few days, just me and maybe a friend.'

'Nothing, boyo, I am sorry. My house is a gallery now. Each of my rooms has become an installation. My own room has nothing, not even a mattress or a sheet. I curl up on the wooden boards.'

'What sort of installation?' I say, repeating the word in his crass Punjabi intonation.

'Art, boyo, where have you been? It's called "Deserted House" and I've smashed the cisterns in the bathroom and torn the wallpaper, leaving corners of it hanging right down into the room with damp and everything. I even put rats in and called in a couple of tramps and gave them some cider for the opening. People turn up every day.'

'What happened to the tramps after opening day?'

'I accused them of stealing my money and handed them over to the police who smacked them good for stealing.'

'How much did they steal?'

'Nothing. A way of losing them. I get new ones when anyone important, reviewers and gallery owners, say they're coming. The whole house is boarded up and we come and go through a loose plank.'

So we went to a hotel and booked a room for the night because she said we might want to move on from there or see what it was like and stay.

She tried the bed out. It was still afternoon so I suggested we see Keats's house and I took her round. We walked back to the hotel and in the room she kissed me. She closed her eyes and stood on tiptoe and held her arms behind her back. She had a vision of herself. Or was she playing the angel I had told her about, the one I was on the lookout for. And she sensed I was uncertain and didn't want to make a grab for her, so she held my face with both her hands.

'So precious,' she said, an adjective that didn't fit.

'I want to lie with you,' she said and she guided me to the bed.

Why did I know it wouldn't work? That I was in a dream and wishing it wasn't that dream. Does one tire of adventure and why then did I resent the way my heart beat when years earlier I would have exulted in the symptom of love?

And when we lay there, because I discovered in a terrifying sweep that there were two kinds of wanting, she got down to what I thought was putting my mind at rest. Making small talk.

'You know TB, don't you?'

'Sure I do.'

'They're shooting at his place, in his house, a party, today,' she said.

'Shooting?'

'An arts documentary. Literature. They're following him round and he's having a party and the Minister for Culture's going.'

'How do you know?'

She'd been reading the magazine of the weekend newspaper. She'd been on the loo. She fetched it.

'So why weren't you invited, Sufi?' Now it emerged, the challenge, the disappointment. She was like a fisherman who has caught the tiddler and wants to throw it back.

'I don't look at London invites any more. I expect Joanna put it on the kitchen dresser and I didn't look at it. Or maybe TB thought we're close enough for him not to send a damned card around, and he probably just rang. Come to think of it, he did say something when I was sponsoring him in Brighton.'

'Then let's go. If you're sure you'd be welcome, I mean.'

'Welcome is not the problem. I was just thinking are we in the mood or should we go for a great dinner and crash out and make plans for tomorrow?'

'We go to the party. I'm in the mood, Sufi.'

I found myself with Lotus in a taxi. I rang Faqr for TB's address. Pakistanis know the phone numbers of famous Pakistanis. Faqr even knew about the party and the documentary.

It was a desperate move, but I was making it – what the hell? The belle on my arm. We got out of the taxi and I went to the door. I ran up the steps of the Notting Hill mansion, partly because I wanted to get to TB before she heard me to remind him who I was and partly because I wanted her to pay the hefty taxi fare, paying which would have cleaned me out.

A Filipino butler answered the door and acted as though he was expecting us. He was expecting everyone, I guess.

Lotus was dressed not only to kill, but to cremate alive, in a simple shiny black dress that was too short and too tight and only had strings to suspend it. It spoke of strings of tautness, of knots and ties beneath.

We were ushered in and the other guests smiled at us, not realizing we were crashers. And then there he was, TB. He looked as though he recognized me but wondered what I was doing reaching for champagne from a tray at his party. I was going to tough it out but I didn't have to. He saw Lotus on my arm and his face melted into a smile.

'So glad you could make it, and ...' Yes, he wanted to be introduced. He was bowing and almost scraping. I wasn't giving in that easily. He'd have to sweat.

'How great to see you man,' he said, shamelessly feasting his eyes on her.

'You're not seeing me, you're seeing her. Lotus, TB, more deadly than the disease,' I said.

'Blunt as ever and full of the old ones, our Sufi. Poets are always more economical with their insults. I'd love to introduce you to another poet or two. I expect Sufi is bored with them or owes them money or vice versa. I'm borrowing Lotus.'

And so saying he was gone.

And so was she.

A fellow wanders up to me.

'Hi, I'm Robert. I've seen you somewhere before. At Hay on Wye on the editor's panel? You are in poetry, aren't you?'

'I am, but I've never been to Way on Hye,' I say.

'Which publisher do you work for? The scene is so down, isn't it? Tons and tons of trash comes through, don't you find ...'

'I am not an editor, I am a poet,' I say.

'Oh, with which publisher?'

'None yet,' I say and he loses interest immediately and looks over my shoulder and says, 'A man more binned against than binning. Excuse me.' He glides off. A line he has prepared to keep down poets of no repute. But then it's like that. I look around. The writers, the artists, the aspirants looking for attention and the next woman.

A black poet I am vaguely acquainted with sidles up to me.

'Oh Sufi, Sufi, look at them, just look at them,' he says. 'Before I won the prize, they would never have invited me. They patronize me as though it was what I was looking for, as though my quest has come to an end,' he says.

'I am amazed that you won a prize. What was it?' I ask. 'And I am even more amazed that you think you need an invitation. I thought you led a charmed life and came to parties without. And the final shock is that your quest has come to an end. I thought you were eternally wedded to the search for inter-racial sex.'

He too drifted away, but without a prepared line, looking straight ahead and smiling broadly at no one in particular.

The cameras were crowding round the Minister of Culture who had arrived with three young men who were her minders. They were groomed like the fellows who advertise clothes in glossy magazines, but didn't have the looks to match.

Then I saw the instruments of vanity and derision. There were TV monitors set up in each room to show the guests what the camera was doing at that point, who was being flavour of the moment. TB was laughing and holding the Minister of Culture round the waist, while Lotus hung on his other arm.

There's not more to tell, not much more of this humiliation, of my delusions and the fall. I caught a glimpse of her every five minutes on the monitors because she didn't leave TB's elbow, the slut. And when they were off the cameras for half an hour, in fact when I thought the cameras had packed up, I stalked the house, went to the top floor bedroom, pretending to look for a toilet and found them. It was a little room with a chaise longue in tiger-skin plastic, a sloping wall and a small bed in which they were going through agonies. A semi-darkened room. I hear voices. I push and the door gives.

'Shut that fucking door,' he shouts from the bed.

'The adjective doesn't go with the door,' I say and retreat.

I stumble into the Notting Hill night.

How could I have hypnotized myself so? How could I have been so cruel to Joanna?

No, I am not the milkman, nor was meant to be.

Not having slept, I was a bit grumpy with the postman when he asked me to sign for the registered letter.

In the envelope was a thing for Sufi. He was gone, there was no reason not to go through his post. It was a contract. For something called 'Brown Girls don't Sing the Blues'. It was from a recording company that had bought the archives of KarmaSounds, defunct, late of the seventies, and was now using one of the songs. It all sounded vaguely familiar. The letter stated that if they had finally tracked down Sufi, they had money for him. It was royalties on the song he had written in the seventies. Could he sign all three copies and return, please. I signed and returned. I knew his signature well enough. I used it on his credit card slips.

Two days later there came a cheque for seven thousand pounds.

Wallop! Who needs Sufi?

The lodgers had all gone home for the hols. I was all alone in the house.

Trailfinders. At last. My first thought was India. Behrampore. I was going to see great-great granny's grave and I was taking her paintings with me and making comparisons. I must get my hair cut short. I don't want to look like the sitcom actress if they've got BBC programmes running on satellite which I believe they go for in a big way. I don't want Indians come up in the street and ask me if I am the funny woman.

Lotus is back the next morning. She comes into the hotel room.

'They've got my cards as payment guarantee for the room, so I didn't want to leave you stranded, my darling,' she says.

'You didn't want to leave me stranded? What about at the party?'

'You were acting like you wanted to go and I found a lot of interesting people about, so I stayed, what's wrong with that?'

'We have no cause to talk about wrong and right,' I said.

All I wanted to know was if she had or hadn't.

'We can kiss and make up,' she said.

'I must stop kissing and wake up,' I said.

'You're sulking.'

'Sulking? Why? Have I lost the million-pound quiz at the first question? Look at you: young, perfect body, features that speak of immortal genes. And me? A suitcase full of verses. Some good, some indifferent, who's to judge? And a game I got drawn into ... and I must go.'

She says 'hush' and holds me and I'm trembling, but I know she knows she made a hasty decision coming here and holing up with me.

'I don't want you to leave. I was only playing around at the party. OK, so what if I let him. It'll be something to tell my friends, won't it?'

'Describe it, millimetre by millimetre, to them. But spare me.'

'But I want to stay with you. Look I've got money, Sufi. Let's hire a cottage in the hills, there must be some hills somewhere – Wales, Scotland, I'll do the cooking and cleaning and we can watch TV at nights, but you write. Finish the epic. I'd want to do that with you, be the instrument.'

'The epic? The epic is my life. But it'll have to wait. Now can we say goodbye without the foolishness of a kiss?'

'What's foolish about a kiss?'

'Nothing. I'm too old to be jealous, or even to have rivals. And you? You're a dream and a poetic lift and a designer woman and you're a stupid American girl with your own hunger for fine feeling and for fame. May you be blessed or cursed with it. Not a web in which I can play the fly – Goodbye. Sweet lady, Goodbye, goodbye.'

'Even *I* know that's Hamlet,' she says.

I clap my hands slowly.

'Of course you do. It's a trap for American litt. vultures. And for people who want to know a symbol when they see one.'

She didn't try to stop me. Or kiss me.

Behrampore 21st June.

They say the monsoon is staying late. I knew nothing of the seasons but the earth seems to be in a springy mood. 'B' itself is in a glade and as filthy as any other Indian town. And this is where I have come to look for Great Great Grandma Mottram. If she is dust into dust, she picked a particularly dusty spot. The town rapidly turns into hutments and long mud walls which enclose the ruins of old British Raj bungalows, roofless ruins most of them and still people live in them. Busy as hives.

And so finally to shame. The graveyard is desecrated. A goat feeds on the graves. The church is a shell and the stones have fallen into it from the walls, the timbers of the roof rotten and burnt. A side which has fallen over is patched with corrugated iron sheeting. Weeds through the floor. It makes me weep. Is this what they lived and died for? Is this the glory that was the Raj? Some of the stones are standing. Malaria, smallpox, this one eighteen years old, that one twelve, this lad twenty.

Anne Mottram's grave has other headstones lying on it. I have to search for her name. The stone marks no spot as it lies horizontal but it still retains the engraving, exactly as great-great grandpa has it in his book.

This is a wonderful country.

All this way to a grave and to a place where the past means nothing. It's not their past. The people that live here ask for rupees. An urchin asks for pounds. In English. He says, 'Mummy, give me pound.'

There's a dog stuck to a bitch – making love in the heat and rain of this graveyard. She who fought to preserve India for posterity. May the ensuing litter prosper!

Faqr takes me in. Does he need to hire a tramp in one of his installations? No, he says, but he needs a security guard at night. The place has become so valuable that vandals want to get in. I remind him that the point of the place is that it's smashed up and anyone who does damage will be assisting the art. He sneers. Security is all. He'll pay me to stay and prevent real damage and vandalism.

I stay awake at nights, on a mattress I have dragged to the front door and listen to the radio. One night a female voice sings, long and melancholy:

'Roll me a joint and pour me some booze
I'm not going to cry
Or threaten to die
Tired of winning and happy to lose
Brown girls don't sing the blues ...'

I know the tune. And then I realize it's my tune. And immediately some arsehole intrudes into the song and does a boogooboogoo rap, a braggart talking incoherent nonsense and then back to my tune again. That's it: *My* tune. My lyrics. No, I am not asleep. I wait for the song to get over. The DJ says it's the latest hit from some Indian bitch with a Yorkshire accent. The latest hit? It's my song. It was written in 1974. Not the bits with the black fellow singing, *'Woola woola woola, I did her on the floor and she begged for more'* or whatever. This guy means it; there is no irony better than the one that is unapprehended.

I wait for the morning and track down the record label in the Kilburn Woolworths and phone the company. Yes, they know what I am talking about and they've sent me three cheques already and congratulations! Is there a problem?

No problem. I was going home. I ask Faqr for my wages.

'What will I do for a night watchman?'

'Let the tramps smash it up. It'll get you even more money when they set fire to it. Do a video of the fire.'

In Brighton the house is locked. She has left a parcel for me. It contains the slim hardback volume of *Gray's Elegy*.

She has written in an impatient, scrawled, accusing hand:

'Full many a flower – under your hairy nose, you insensitive, lying bastard. Goodbye.'

I search the house. Her Indian archive is gone.

The bank! Yes, she has cashed the cheques from our joint account. Seven thousand pounds and rising.

Blessed are they who sing 'Woola woola woola' and the rest.

'I'll take that money you think you owe me,' I tell Willie. He is surprised to see me.

'I thought you'd emigrated, but I'm glad you're back, man. The faculty want to give me another contract. More Living Poetry man. I'll give you half, sixty per cent ... '

I tell him I have to make momentous decisions. He generously hands over the cash.

In Delhi, I go to the Archaeological Survey of India building. It is grand and dusty as is everything in official India, giving off the air of campers in territory they have occupied. Only the bureaucracy, the endless old files, seemed at home in the dusty environment. There were splashes and streaks of red spit in every corner of every building. Indians spit everywhere and if one points it out, they deny all knowledge of spitting and spit in your face. I patiently explain my query to one clerk after another, one official after another. It has become a litany.

'I have traced my great-great grandmother's grave in Behrampore. I have been there and discovered this beautiful seventeenth-century garrison church and the graveyard in ...' and so on and on. I would end with the tempting suggestion that if something were done it would be a neat and magnetic attraction for tourists, European and American and possibly Indian. I was throwing in stuff about respect for the past. By the end of the first day, I could rattle this lecture off in my sleep.

They would hear me out.

'You do one thing, you come tomorrow,' one said, as he handed me back the photographs I had taken of the state of the place.

'And what happens tomorrow?'

'I will not be here. Mr Rao will be here in this chair.'

He smiles.

'No, I will not come tomorrow. I demand to speak to someone now. Someone responsible. The last fellow heard me out and said he was "Ancient Hindu" and I wanted "Raj". Now you tell me to come tomorrow. Who bloody runs this place? And what do you all do? I can't believe you sit around here all day, all year and can't give me a simple answer about ... you were reading the newspaper and scratching your ... well whatever when I came in, what do you do? Who is in charge? Why can't anyone give me an answer in this damned department? I have been here four days running and been pushed from one idiot to another.'

'You are too insulting madam and saying unlady like things about scratching. Very nasty, bad.'

The fans on the ceiling whirr. I have made a fool of myself. I'll get nowhere with this attitude. I must use charm if I can summon it. I have intruded into this office through sheer bloody-mindedness. The man who showed me in has disappeared and now this poor fellow is stuck with a raving, white woman whose diatribe is making everyone, even the clerks who seem to be contemplating old ledgers, uncomfortable.

'Perhaps I can help,' says a very smooth voice. I turn round to see a middle-aged man, very fashionably dressed in baggy khaki shirt and trousers behind me.

'I was told you were here. I am Harish Aurora, Preservation. I know all about the De Braganca church in Behrampore.'

I stood up. I was amazed. I had been floundering around for three days in the depths of these departments and finally I'd scored a bullseye.

'The Braganca church. You know about it.'

'It's my job ma'am. Interesting, late Indo-Iberian. Much after Goa and Bombay.'

'You're real,' I say. 'I am going to reach out and touch you. Don't disappear.'

He smiles.

'Please,' he says, indicating the door. 'I heard about you yesterday and was hoping you'd come back. My office is in another building, but I was told yesterday, at an evening party actually, about a young, white woman who is parading photographs of Behrampore around the ministry and getting very angry.'

'Not so young,' I say.

The gardens of the ministry are perfectly maintained. We walk across to the car park.

'Would you care to join me for a drink and tell me about your mission which I have some inkling of? My office is hardly a place to sit and talk. Scribblers all round.'

We go to something called The Habitat Centre, a red-brick complex which looks for all the world like a British Polytechnic or the faculty building of some new university.

'More Archaeological Survey?'

'No, it's a club, believe it or not, with rooms to live in and places to eat and drink. The chattering classes of Delhi.'

Everyone seems to know Harish Aurora in this building.

When he fetches me a very welcome drink, fending off waiters who offer to do it for him, I show him my photographs. I mustn't vent my indignation on him.

'Yes, a disgrace. I studied architecture. Our De Braganca was a remarkable fellow. Soldier, builder, designer, artist. It's a lovely little church. But there's no money to restore it. There's hope. Some industry is coming into the town and I may be able to tap them for some cash, but the government, this government, any government, doesn't care. Not a toss.'

I tell him about my quest when he gets round to enquiring what my beef is. He is amazing. He knows the name Mottram. He actually knows and has read about my great-great grandfather. He doesn't know the wife as well. He knows she was a painter and restorer and helped her husband set up the very department of which he is now a grand official.

'In the John Lockwood Kipling gang. He started my business – restoration. And of course his wife Anne. All of them, but I didn't know she ended up in Behrampore? Tch tch, it's my patch. Stupid me. You see, we Indians don't really believe that things in books happen on the ground. We don't really trust maps. Books are books, reality is reality. Well, well, well! His great-great granddaughter?'

I tell him that I have Anne Mottram's paintings, the whole portfolio of watercolours, pencil drawings and sketches of the monuments that his department handles.

He says he would give the little finger of his right hand to see them and I vouchsafe that that particular sacrifice will not be called for.

I meet him again that evening and together we look at the hundred or so pictures.

'I am going to slap a preservation order on these, Joanna. I am sorry. The department will confiscate them. You can't take these paintings out of the country.'

'Then I shan't be your friend,' I say.

'In which case, of course, I'll let the matter rest, turn a blind eye. Better that history suffers than I do.'

He was charming. The next day he showed me two churches and a mosque in the environs of Delhi which were off the tourist track and perfect little pieces of building. He pointed to the peculiarities of each.

I tell him that I plan to tour India, to see the Taj and then progress on the same journey that Anne Mottram took with her husband, the grand restorer.

He nods. He is thoughtful. He wants my itinerary. I show him the map in Anne's diary and he smiles.

'I wanted to follow it as closely as possible,' I say.

'The towns have been renamed. There are highways where there were no roads at the time, and of course railways and airports in the tiniest places. We can get to Agra in twenty minutes. Or on the train in less than four hours.'

I noticed he said 'we'. So deliberate, he wanted me to notice.

He must have mentally memorized the map in those few minutes, because that evening, when I returned from my own wanderings by rickshaw, there was a package waiting for me. It had a route map neatly drawn. So the architect had emerged. And it had a very easy-to-follow timetable of planes and trains and a schedule of guesthouses and hotels. He hadn't given me his home phone number, so I waited till the next morning and was going to call him at his office, when he called me. From the hotel lobby.

I was having coffee and thought it not indecent to invite him up. What was I flattering myself for? He is a suave, undoubtedly committed family man? If anything, his virtue and reputation needed preserving.

'Thanks, that's all very useful and these guesthouses?'

'I was going to make an offer. If I am with you, we can stay at these government guesthouses, as guests. I have work, restoration work, by great coincidence in all the places that you've marked on the map. The Palace at Udaipur, the small Imambara in Lucknow, the garrison church in Meerut, Shaniwarwada in Pune, or Poona as our great-great grandma called it, and so on.'

'You are going to follow me around through that whole tour? Why?'

'Work, a whim, a passion – for old buildings. And it'll stir me out of my laziness, I was supposed to go round and visit them any way. But don't worry, I'll be in and out of Delhi. You'll do the tour, I'll join you now and then if you will permit me.'

'That would be very nice.'

'Then let my secretary book the planes and when there's a good train ride, the trains. Like Bombay to Poona which you must do by *Deccan Queen*. It's the name of a train. Like your famous *Flying Scotsman*.'

'But that's so much trouble for you.'

'It's a pleasure. One pleasure after a long time.'

'Tell me about the last time.'

'When we're on our way,' he says.

Turkmenistan Airlines is a bad way to go. It makes unscheduled stops in Sofia, Ankara, Samarkand, Dushanbey and Kabul. They said it was a direct flight. Then Delhi, and no permission to land. We circle because we are two days late. Yes they've given us three meals, but in as many days. The aircraft has turned unsavoury, stale, stinking. Everyone ties hankies around their faces, like the bandanas of the outlaws in Westerns and the flight looks like its made up of hijackers. The steward knows I am a poet. In a weak moment I confessed. He wants me to write a poem about the flight and the sweet scent of heaven that embraces the craft. Joker.

Harish is on the same plane, though he said he wouldn't be. Last-minute change of plan. His office had been told that he was urgently required in Udaipur. We drive from the airport to the Lake Palace Hotel and a reception committee awaits us.

'This is not the rough-and-ready government guesthouse you booked me in. Shall I take the cab on?' I ask.

'Another small change of plan. You have been invited to stay here. The government guesthouse is booked up by some minister's relatives.'

The manager and assistant manager and their flunkies are all 'yes, Mr Aurora' and 'no, Mr Aurora' to Harish.

At the reception the manager asks which room we'd like.

'I'd like the cheapest,' I say. 'I don't mind what view it has.'

'You are a guest of the ministry,' Harish says.

'Don't be ridiculous, I am no such thing.'

'The Prithvi Suite, sir?'

'That would be nice,' says Harish.

'But I've told you what I want.'

'And a room close by for Joanna.'

'Mrs Akhtar,' I say.

'Shall we meet in the lobby when you've settled in? Half an hour? I can point you in several directions for the rest of the day.'

He is sensitive and knows when to withdraw. My god what am I saying, or thinking! The Big A. Water the milk. Harish's ministry must be very important because they are laying everything on – the car to the palaces, bottles of wine in refrigerated boxes, luxury hampers for picnics ...

The sandstone of the fort hasn't changed colour for a hundred and fifty years. Anne Mottram has captured the peculiar shade of pinkish sandstone in watercolours and almost perfectly the shade of orange of the sunset behind the canopied battlements with their rounded umbrellas and the melancholy elaboration of their iron-studded doorways. It's precise, exquisite, fussy even.

'This is our pride and joy. Rajasthan on the whole is well-preserved,' says Harish and leaves me wanting him to explain why.

Outside the palace, a man with a birdcage with ten singing birds comes to us. He wants to sell us the birds. He has smaller empty cages in which he'll put them – the takeaway cages – if we care to buy.

'That's much too cruel.' The words escape me.

'Their cage or his poverty?' Harish asks.

'The country not providing him with another way of earning a living,' I say.

'His father trapped birds before him and maybe his great-great grandfather trapped them for the king who lived in the palace. This is what our wonderful democracy has reduced him to, selling to tourists.

'I am going to buy them,' I say. 'How much?'

'For one?'

'For all ten.'

The man looks at Harish as though to ask if I am serious. The hotel's chauffeur who has brought us here, steps up.

'If an insolent price so much as passes your lips, I'll see to your mother and sister,' he says in Hindi to the man.

The man gets the message.

'Give me what you like.'

'Give him two hundred rupees, on the minimum wage principle,' says Harish. The transaction puzzles him, but he won't ask why I want ten birds.

I hand over the money, take the birdcage and, walking up to the clump of trees past the car park, set them loose. One by one the birds take wing and get to the branches. I throw the cage down and stamp on it; it hurts my foot and doesn't do the cage too much damage.

As we leave in the car, I can see the birdman with a group of taunting urchins who have followed this drama behind him, picking up the cage and whistling at the little multicoloured song-birds in the branches above.

It was called the *October Journal* and the picture I remember most clearly was the Taj Mahal on a full moon night. I know Joanna. She'll arrive at the Taj Mahal when it's full moon in October, this month. I only have to check a calendar to see when that will be and make my way to Agra.

I got Willie to fax my six published poems to my old friend C.P. Leela, the poet, and to tell him of my impending arrival and get him to alert the world of poetry.

Leela was not at the airport to receive me. Well, how could he be? The flight landed two days late. I took a taxi to Leela's house. I needed a bath.

He was good to me. He said that the world of poetry had been alerted.

'That's great. And?'

'And they are very indifferent as to your comings and goings.'

To speak frankly, he had shown a girl at the British Council my poems and she had agreed to sponsor, at short notice, a small reading of my work, providing Leela also joined me on the bill. He was willing to do me this favour for old times' sake.

Only five people came to the reading and three of them were British Council staff. Leela introduced me to the audience saying that my latest triumph was in the world of Indi-pop which had just released my 70's hit 'Brown girls and something about their sadness' – this was as close as he could get to my dynamo title '*Brown Girls Don't Sing the Blues*'. Apart from which ... and he told them about my epic, the work in progress. I had brought my own manuscript but, even as I read it, it didn't make much sense to me. After half an hour I paused.

'I want to share something peculiar with this audience,' I said. ' I haven't been back home to India for over twenty years now and somehow language changes when you land in the subcontinent. Sentences seem to take on their own shapes ...'

The audience suddenly woke up. This, they wanted to hear.

'The lines sound different to me. And frankly what made perfect sense in Brighton seems ridiculous here. That's the word, I think: "ridiculous". I think I've wasted half an hour of your time and squandered some of your goodwill. You must forgive me. Think of it this way: I've wasted twenty years of my own.'

Yes, I move in with Harish for the second night. I spend the first one wondering why I hadn't. I keep the room on, just to be discreet and not to tempt fate. I don't tell him that I haven't made love for ten years or maybe more. He is gentle with me.

Why does he want me? I don't need an answer to the question, but the question won't go away. I have asked him nothing about himself and he has obliquely volunteered the information that, though he is married and has children, he is a free agent. He is not all that young, perhaps the same age as Sufi and me, but he is athletic, intelligent, professional, even rich. If he is unencumbered as he implies, he can find a million Indian girls, and for that matter a clutch of the foreign girls that come and go from and live in Delhi.

And I am ashamed, even as we make love. That he is with a woman past her fiftieth? Does he need this? But I need it and I am going to be greedy.

He sleeps soundly and snores after. I lie awake and it's then that I know that I must do this tour, fulfil this purpose. I have Sufi's Indi-pop money in notes and traveller's cheques, deposited so that I can pull it out with an international Visa card when I want. He hasn't supported me for nigh on thirty years and now he's rich, but he's gone, and I've got his money. Harish snores. I look at his body in the moonlight, drawing back the curtains. Perfectly brown, curled like an embryo in sleep, small bums and hairy only on his arms below the elbow. Some girls would give ... Who cares? He wants me.

He has done this for a bet. The thought strikes me – like *Guys and Dolls*. Someone in his office, in his ministry. He's bet them that he can seduce this silly old English woman, the one who berated the babu for scratching his balls. After all, white women only come on their own to India to sample the brown.

And maybe he's not ministry at all, just the man who took the bet and then read up the rest and fooled me with it – architect, church, Beharampore, de Braganca – and he's won. Or maybe he bet that he can get me to a hotel in Udaipur, just like Sky Masterson in *Guys and Dolls* got the wretched Salvationist to go with him to Cuba.

And the hotel staff is in on it! What have I done?

I collect my stuff from my room and at the reception I ask for the bill, I'm checking out. The man gives me a bill for three hundred rupees.

I pay it and as I hand over the notes, I calculate. That's five pounds fifty. There's a mistake in the bill. He's left a couple of zeroes out.

'There's a mistake,' I say.

'No mistake madam, three hundred rupees,' says the clerk.

'For two nights?'

'What to do madam. If you want bill, you got a bill. We are not charging Mr Aurora's guests.'

'But I don't want to be Mr Aurora's guest.'

'How can you say that if he says to us you are?'

'But why don't you charge me, even if I am his guest?'

'He is our father and mother,' says this clerk.

'I didn't know we were in a hurry,' says Harish from behind me. He has dressed and dashed down.

'I had better leave,' I say. 'But they don't want to charge me.'

'What did I do wrong?' Harish asks. 'Have just one coffee with me. Give me one more chance. How have I offended you? I agree I must have, but I have no idea how, which is also my fault.'

'Shut your whining, Harish,' I say irritated that the two desk clerks are listening to this. Is this part of the deal, the bet? That he humiliates me. 'Let's have your coffee.'

We walk to the breakfast room and I know I'm wrong. There's no bet. He is, archaeologically speaking, 'Preservation'.

He limps, spiritually limps from the wound, and my heart goes out to him. I have confused him with my paranoia.

Over coffee he regains his composure. He is suave. Probably well travelled and certainly experienced in the neuroses of women. He fancies himself as a handler, a tamer. I have to know what he thought of my behaviour. Had he put it down to old woman jitters and if he had, how blooming dare he!

'Do you pay all your "guests'" bills? Whoever they are. Whites I presume.'

'I swear on my mother's life, or the emperor's tomb , may it crumble tomorrow, I haven't brought a woman here before. Do you believe me, Joanna? These clerks talk in that way, they screw up. "Mr Aurora's guests". They don't know what they're saying. I could kill the bastards. They've screwed it up for me by giving you this crass impression'

'No they haven't,' I say, and smile. 'But I insist on paying my own bill. I have the money. Ill-gotten gains. My ex-husband's earnings from a pop song.'

'Well, let's be grown-up about this. I shall never suggest sleeping with you again, though it revived my youthful dreams and passions, and we can be travelling companions?'

'No. You tell me why you wanted to sleep with me in the first place.'

Only later on the thought crossed my mind that he had the answer worked out.

'Shorthand: Portuguese architecture, the Indo-Iberian canon, a real appreciation of the Indian light and colour. Do you think Indian women care about these things? Or any woman I have met seems to me a soul mate? Like you instantly are?'

I fell for it.

And so on to Dholpur, where the palace is empty, falling apart and locked up and even when it's opened up for us, pretty unimpressive. But Harish takes me by his ministry jeep to an old abandoned hunting lodge by a lake in a game reserve. The hunting lodge is empty, deserted, but Harish has ordered string beds with mattresses and a portable kitchen, a fridge, basins, pumps, everything. There's even a cook attached and all of it arrives by truck and is set up by six servants, just for us.

The lodge was built by the Maharaja of Dholpur for the purpose of hunting and making love and it's now empty. It has one storey, high-ceilinged rooms with balconies overlooking the lake. This is where we live for five idyllic days, watching the deer and the birds, the wild boar, snakes and tortoises who drink from the lake.

'I must count the calendar days to the full moon,' I say and show him the painting of the Taj. He says the tradition is to sight the Taj by moonlight and to kiss. So we honour the tradition. Even though it's only in a painting.

The car that Harish had sent for me was stopped by a procession crossing the road. A curious sight. Twenty or so men, some in rags, some in the urban uniform of the Indian worker, all tied to each other by loose nooses around their necks with rope binding their left hands to each other, were being walked in a crocodile by six policemen.

And there, fifth from the front was Sufi. He was in a shirt and khaki trousers and wore his brown shoes. He held his head high, as though this wasn't happening to him, as though the public who half-noticed this procession of shame weren't jeering. I stopped the taxi and leapt out. I screamed, but he didn't hear me. The police stopped anyone getting near their merry band and marched them down an alley which they blocked off. I ran back to the car and asked the chauffeur what that was.

'No ticket madam. Train ticket. Going without train ticket, rascals.'

'With ropes round their necks? For dodging fares? Where have they taken them?'

'Don't worry madam, police will beat them mercilessly.'

'They'll beat them?'

'First slaps and then taking in magistrate court.'

'Take me to the magistrate's court. Now.'

'Harish sahab said bring to madam in Taj hotel.'

'Doesn't matter what Harish sahab said.'

It didn't look anything like a courtroom. There were a few men sitting at a table and hordes of people milling about, not in the least interested in the proceedings before the bench. I walked in and found myself at the back of the crowd. Sufi was there, with two policemen round him, looking very hot and bothered and red in the face. He didn't see me.

The magistrate asked him his name.

'Sufi Akhtar.'

The magistrate looked up.

'My god, no! Are you a poet?'

'Yes,' said Sufi, not in the least alarmed or interested that this magistrate in Agra had some clue as to his identity.

'Were you published by Poet's Workshop in Delhi?'

'Yes.'

'Oh yes,' says the magistrate and grins. '*Buggered, beggared and abandoned, Mountbatten's hasty retreat, Leaving us to our anger and our flame, The trains of mutilation and death, Crossing boundaries ...*'

Sufi is amazed. The only man who has ever quoted his own verse back at him. The clerk looks at the magistrate.

'So what were you doing, Mr Akhtar? Did you lose your ticket?'

'I did.'

'You were sitting in first class?'

'Yes.'

'Without intentionality to defraud?'

'No intentionality at all.'

'That is fine. The case is dismissed. Only one formality, you have to supply address to be released as non-vagrant. You have a hotel?'

'No, and no money to get one. The railway police robbed me.'

'This is very irregular, Mr Akhtar, but maybe I will have to use my address for you, failing any other solution or hotel.'

'The Taj Mughal. He is with me in that hotel, use my room number. I am his wife,' I pipe up. I want to say 'It's me, Sufi, Joanna.' Sufi looks in my direction. A tear falls down his cheek. He must be tired, poor sod.

'Will you have a private word with me afterwards, Mr Akhtar?' asks the magistrate.

'Call me Sufi, your Honour,' says Sufi, largely relieved that fate has taken a hand. For once his poem has done him some good. But maybe he knows about the pop song taking off too and now he turns to hurry out of hell. But does he want to acknowledge me? I sign the address and release paper.

He tells me he calculated our rendezvous by the moon.

We are sitting by the swimming pool and this joker comes up.

'My husband,' Joanna says.

'My God! Harish Aurora. I don't believe it.'

'Sufi,' he says and looks at Joanna. 'You never told me.'

'Told you what? You know each other? Obviously. Why am I fooling myself?'

'Sufi and I were in school together in the hills, before his family became rabidly Muslim and moved to Pakistan,' Harish says.

'True, but even before I went we used to read Jack Kerouac together and dreamt of hitting the road, yes?'

'Dreams, which you fulfilled I believe,' says Aurora. 'England, poetry, the abandonment of all bourgeois aspirations like marriage and mortgages.'

'Excuse me, Sufi has both. And has had for over thirty years,' says Joanna. 'Now things may be different.'

I don't know what to say to that. The Lotus business is still bothering her. We have said nothing about it.

'He has a very beautiful new young woman,' she says.

'I'd like to talk to you, but without this clown listening,' I say.

'Shall I help you into the pool, Sufi, to cool off?' Aurora says.

I start to laugh.

'Your threats never meant much did they, Harish? So what do you do now? Sell nylon franchises to Singapore?'

'I serve art in my small way, Sufi. I am an employee of the Archaeological Survey of India.'

'Hence the interest in old monuments,' I say. I don't mean to say it and look at Joanna with a grin, but the punch and counterpunch of the eternal battle between us has made this sort of remark a reflex action. It just flows without thought.

'Was Miss Bimbo also caught ticketless, or did you trade her in a Bombay bazaar?' Joanna asks.

'I have blundered into landmine territory with no interest in the present battle,' says Harish. 'Sufi, it's very sad that after all these years we can't have a drink together. Maybe when you and Joanna have settled who is with whom?'

'Boys, this is monumentally silly,' says Joanna.

'Find me in the bar,' the fellow says and goes.

'You have no right to barge in on my trip like this,' says Joanna.

'You know, I have the feeling that when you tell this story of Agra it will be all about how you saved me from the magistrate.'

'No it won't. Your poem saved you.'

'Ah, a new respect for the truth.'

'I don't need any of this, Sufi. You didn't reply. Where's your little American bimbo? Can she get your thing excited or have you come to India because the Viagra's on the black market?'

'Both. And how about old Aurora, does he have to strap on a splint?'

'Very satisfactory,' she says. It hurts.

'Keep him. He was always an idiot. I came for the money you stole,' I say.

'That's rich. If we got a proper separation, I'd get the house and more than fifty per cent of your royalties. I was the main breadwinner in that rusty, diseased, parasitic relationship.'

I get up and start to leave and she runs after me.

She thrusts two thousand rupees on me.

'Sufi, it's all I've got. I didn't mean to take your money. I don't want to stop you, but where are you going?'

'None of your business,' I say, taking the cash.

'Is she with you? Are you going to tell me? But I suppose that too is none of my business. Now that I am with Harish.'

She said that deliberately.

I found myself a flea-pit hotel in the bazaar area with the money.

I look at the map, sitting by the poolside. I haven't slept all night and Harish, who has promised that we shall travel together to Behrampore so I can tell him what I think should be done with great-great gran's graveyard, keeps throwing his legs about and pressing his erections against me in his sleep.

I have coffee in the room early morning. All caution has been thrown to the winds. Who cares what the butlers think?

Harish joins me wearing a white towelling dressing gown, the hotel's property from behind the bathroom door. He rubs his eyes and answers the phone.

'No I don't want to see them,' he says.

They, whoever they are, ring again.

'I said no,' says Harish.

While he is in the shower there is a knock at the door and one of the senior hotel staff asks to enter. He is with two guys carrying baskets.

'Some fruit for Mr Aurora. He is expecting it.'

'He'll be out in a minute.'

'That's all right,' says the hotel man and the other two gentlemen deposit the baskets, two-feet high each of them, smile and are gone.

Harish looks at the baskets when he comes out of the shower drying his hair with a towel, naked, brown, beautiful, vain.

He looks at the baskets and takes the lid off one.

'Mangoes?' I ask. 'I thought the season was over.'

He doesn't reply but delves in the basket and pulls out a jewellery box. He opens it. There is a gold necklace in it, immodest but exquisite.

'For you,' he says.

'For me? You didn't order that for me?'

'Yes, it *is* a bit much,' he says.

'Who're those guys?'

Harish doesn't reply.

'Well, I don't accept it,' I say. I tell him I'm going to sit by the pool before the sun gets too hot.

He follows me to the pool and orders breakfast. I am looking at his carefully drawn map.

'Behrampore is quite close,' I say. 'I didn't realize.'

'Not all that close,' says Harish. 'It's a very bad road. It'll take hours. And you've already been there. Agra is great!

And the Taj, you haven't seen the Taj yet. That's my great treat.'

'I thought we'd take a day trip to B and then do the Taj tomorrow.'

'It'll take longer than that,' he says.

An old man with ramrod dignity, wearing a blazer with a red hanky sticking out of its pocket, approaches us. Harish stands up to greet him and then I recognize him. The magistrate.

'Good to see you, Harish. News reached you had hit town. But really I am looking for Mrs Akhtar from last morning. How are you, madam?'

'Fine, but the truth is I don't know where Sufi is,' I say.

'Has he gone shopping?'

'I really don't know,' I say.

'But he will be back?'

'That too I can't say.'

He is puzzled. He doesn't want to push the questions any further.

He sits down.

'So Harish. The Behrampore development is on?'

'We are thinking about it,' says Harish. He is clearly uncomfortable and wants to steer away from the subject. I can see the cat coming out of the bag, clambering out quite rapidly.

'What do you mean, thinking, boy? Your contractors swore their affidavits last week. The bulldozers will be moving there now. It will do the district immense good. You have made those buggers very happy.'

The rupee drops. Harish looks like a cornered fox.

'These bulldozers, magistrate sahab, Behrampore. What are they doing?'

'Harish must have told you. Some useless colonial buildings and things, ruins really, old graves and things that nobody cares for. All under Harish's department. He is doing great works. Modernizing.'

'We should go today,' I say to Harish. 'I'd love to see the bulldozers in action. Shall I wear the gold necklace you gave me, or is it dangerous – dacoits and bandits.'

'No, nothing. Nothing like that,' says the magistrate. 'Wear whatever you like. Those days are gone. We've cleaned up the place. No dacoits. Perfect law and order.'

'But there must still be some corruption. Bribery, developers, contractors, land-grabbers making deals. Officials accepting gifts, gold necklaces, mangoes.'

'Yes, yes, that is always there,' says the magistrate. 'This is India.'

I am in the process of packing when Harish walks into the room. He is cool, brazen.

'So you're rushing to judgement,' he says. 'No questions? No innocent till proven guilty?'

'What are your paymasters going to build there?'

'A spa, a hotel. Progress. Look, I was going to try and save them, but the others in my department, my superiors, they've overruled me. So what can I do? Cry? And anyway, British colonial graves – you know what they mean to most Indians? Oppression. The memory of conquest and humiliation. You really think anyone in my department, except myself, sees any purpose in keeping such reminders of our shame?'

'No, no, no, off with their heads! But Harish I thought you agreed with me that the church, the Indo-Iberian little gem in the middle of nowhere, should be preserved.'

I had finished packing, I clamped my suitcase shut and went for the door.

'Where are you going, Joanna? Is my explanation no good? You can't see the Indian point of view? Only the Imperial memory matters?'

'I am going to Behrampore and I'm going to lie down in front of the bulldozers. I learnt the tactic from Gandhi. Heard of him?' I ask.

'Just a minute. Give me one minute for old times' sake,' says Harish.

He gets on the phone. He makes three calls.

'I don't see the point,' I say and he holds up his hand for me to be patient.

'Aurora here. What's the report from the construction camp? The demolition of the stone structure? I see. OK. All right. You are the chief engineer? Do me one favour. Can you save the headstone, you know the stone with writing on top of the grave, just one of them. It's called Anne Mottram. Yes please. Good.'

He turns to me.

'By the time you get there, there'll only be one preserved stone. Joanna, I am not a brute, I am sorry. I'll have the stone brought here, or to Delhi or shipped to London or wherever. You're not going and ending all this, are you?'

I am.

But I want the stone.

I seek out the magistrate in his court.

'"*Buggered, beggared and abandoned*" that is so beautiful. Onomatopoeia,' he says.

'Alliteration,' I say.

'A long time since I did my BA,' he says.

There is to be Urdu poetry at the Taj and I am to be his guest and to bring Mrs Akhtar too. I can't tell him that I am not in touch with Mrs Akhtar. He says he'll send the car round for me at eight. It's a full moon night.

He's going to send his car to the bloody Taj so I have to wait outside the five-star hotel for the car and slip the major-domo twenty rupees to induce him to pretend to treat me like a hotel guest in front of the chauffeur when he arrives. I try and stand in the shadows in case Harish or Joanna, or worse, both together, are entering or leaving the hotel.

The car takes me to the Taj. The monument has been cordoned off by police and only the holders of badges are allowed into the gardens that surround it. The magistrate meets me at the gate and the sound of the poetic chorus, the quwaali, accompanied by drums, harmonium and the clapping troupe, seems distant and hoarse. As we approach the rows of deckchairs on which guests are seated, very many people come up to the magistrate. I am introduced. Meaningless names. Faces in the dark as a cloud passes the moon. I tell the magistrate I must meditate on the lines, no more introductions. He respects that and I set out on my own.

Of course she'd be there. And she knows I will be too.

'I have something for you, Sufi.' She hands me an envelope.

'Divorce papers?'

She smiles.

'Your money, signed travellers' cheques, so be careful.'

'I have something for you too,' I say and hand her the folded sheet of paper from my pocket.

'Too dark, you read it, Sufi,' she says.

I don't need to. I have spent the day composing it.

The monuments she painted stand
O life, O love, O bird in hand,
O beauty that must fly away
How quickly falls the end of day.'

'It's for great-great grandma,' I say.

'It's beautiful. Say it again.'

I repeat it.

'It's competent, but second-rate. And that's what epitaphs should be, I suppose.'

'No, it's just right. But you don't know that the bastards have bulldozed the graveyard? Sold for a bribe. Millions of rupees probably. Anne's ashes raked over for a pleasure park.'

We stroll in the gardens of the Taj.

'I've missed you,' I say. I can say this now that it's half-dark and she can't see the shame that my face must betray.

'I've missed you too.'

'But I was the one who was misled by vanity and greed. It's really all over now. And, Joanna, nothing happened.'

'Forget it. I don't want to know.'

'Is that because one confession deserves another and you don't want to tell me?'

'I said forget it, OK?'

'OK. And I'm glad we're at last in India together. That too was a mistake, not bringing you earlier.'

'Well, it's moonlight, it's the Taj, what more can one ask?'

'Poetry'

'There it is,' she says indicating the quwaali that comes over the breeze. 'What does it say?'

'It says:

"Love may be but a breeze of spring
That carries a seed and lets it grow
The bird of youth is on the wing,
Where shall the birds of winter go?"'

'Does it really say that?' she asks.

'No it doesn't. He is wittering on about his devotion to some saint or the other.'

She laughs by moonlight.

We go back to Sufi's flea-pit. I'll get my things tomorrow, but I am not going back for the gravestone. Who needs it? Let him hang it round his prosaic neck.

e-mailwallahs

C734 Block 13

Lane No. 47, Workers Colony

Shivaji Link Road, Borivili

Bombay

Dear Daddyji,

God protect you and Mataji and our precious jewel Sitambari. I wish I could give better news, but I am conveying only truth. I have no job yet.

I am going every day on the suburb train. Main-line local it is called, into Bombay proper, and attending at the offices which have given advertise in the newspapers for job vacations. I am every day mostly sitting on benches spending waiting time, with some boss then telling that they have no proper vacations for over-qualified gentlemens like me. Sometime I am thinking not to tell them that I am holding my BA and simply to pretend that I am an illiterate swine worthy of doing their humble job. Mostly I think that even will not help because what is going on is that plenty people, mens and womens, are applying for these jobs and only those which are paying the clerk some bribe are getting name on list.

I tried it with ten rupees, I am ashamed to tell you, but God must have been watching because the clerk returned the money and said people are leaving 'big papers' to get this job. I spoke him kindly and said I have no big papers to impart just this moment but after I get the job he could be on percentage basis. He laughed too much. He told that lump sum was preferred and ask me to borrow it, then only I would get an employment in Bombay.

Acting on this peon's advice I approached Kakaji for a small loan. Now, God willing, you have brought me up to believe that people must convey all truth at all times, I wish to state the following. Please believe, Daddyji, this is not with any disrespect for your younger brother who has allowed me into his home and given me a rubber mattress and regular meals and facilities. I am too much grateful, but I must still tell that Kakaji is drinking from bottle all the time, with red eyes and not going to work.

He is also abusing and forgetting who is who. He tells that he loves me and that he loves you as elder brother, but mostly he is abusing the family, the government, his employers who have kicked him out of job and even the Communist union-wallahs who are obtaining suspensions-pay for him from his firm. They are paying something and with that we are surviving, except most is going in bad habits, of which only alcohol I stoop to mention.

Somebody have to explain to Kakaji that this is not the way and I am too small a nephew for doing this task. Please you consider a trip this way.

I shall most certainly obtain a job, hoping sooner but maybe later. I have never forgotten the mission.

Please beg those people, the boy's family, to wait just a few week more and then the wage packet will come into their hands for the dowry and they can start having confidence that we are not a pauper family but can marry our jewel, Sitambari, with honour to their boy.

Please convey to Sitambari that I never cease to remember my little sister and will exert all sinews in her favour.

Bombay is a no good city. I went to the temple to pray that rains don't fail, for our fields that God has given and for you.

Mission will be accomplished, boss. I am Optimister!

Your loving son,
Shyamalam

Bloomsbury Publishers
28 Soho Square London W1

To
Mr Dilip Dilawar Singh
394 C Maharaja Gardens
New Delhi

Dear Mr Dilip Dilawar Singh,

Further to my congratulatory and grovelling e-mail, I introduce myself properly and formally.

You won't mind that Petra showed me the e-mail that you sent her asking about our balance of responsibilities. It is absolutely OK that you ask and necessary that you get an answer straight from the horse's mouth and the horse happens to be yours truly at this end.

So without making a meal of it, my job is to send you the titles and possibly to make suggestions. I can and will give you complete descriptions of the titles we are about to publish so you can sound out your selection sources or decide yourself. It's very clear that I am to be the collaborator in developing the markets worldwide and specifically in the, for us, exciting territory of English-speaking India.

I want to stress that *you* choose from the list, your vast experience in the field, in England, New York and now in India will be invaluable. I am told you are the whiz at getting people to read what they didn't know they wanted to read. You must teach me the trick. I started as a 'PR' rep and learnt a few stunts but never discovered this vital secret.

Hope to hear,
Yours etc.
Sandy

From: BuntyB87@vsnl.com
To: Sandybeech@bloomsburynet.co.uk

Dear Sandy,

I'm going to be e-mailing you and you me every day so we'd better cut the Dilip Dilawar Singh crap. All my mates and even all my enemies (so you don't have to choose which you're going to be) call me Bunty. It isn't flattering but it comes from school when a precocious physics teacher, who thought he was more English than the English, used to refer to us with names from Dickens and the William books and God knows what. You guessed it. He used to call me Bunter and thence Bunty. I must say straight away that I am nothing like the character in the book. For one, I am not fat and I don't wear round glasses – strictly designer Armanis.

Enough of that – I'll end up telling you my shoe size, won't I?

The list of non-fiction you sent me – general reading around the sciences and maths should do very well in India. Can we have a trial run of samples? Send me the twenty titles I have marked.

I wish it were true that I had the gift of opening up magic reading markets. No such skill but some such luck.

I'll let you know how my preliminary investigations go.

Yours, just

Bunty

From: Sandybeech@bloomsburynet.co.uk

To: BuntyB87@vsnl.com

Dear Bunty,

Yes I think we can dispose of your real name, though I do think it's very impressive – Dilip Dilawar Singh sounds much more impressive than John Smith or even Sandra Beech. That's why the Sandy – even though it's a double 'e' and not 'ea', get it?

Yes, the maths books seem a great idea.

The Philosophy Of Maths is probably the worst possible title they could have chosen, but that's up to editorial and they pretend to consult us but they go their own sweet way. But I assure you the book itself is a cracking read. I am sending you the reviews we've had of it here. Enthusiastic to say the least. I've also ringed the other titles in the faxed list which ought to get to you pronto.

Ever,

Sandy

From: BuntyB87@vsnl.com

To: Sandybeech@bloomsburynet.co.uk

Dear Sandy,

E-mailing this from Bombay. I flew over to meet our reps here and then your pronto got interrupted by the damned postal strike. There's no way round that one if you've already sent the consignment. I'll just have to go back to Delhi and wait the term out. One never knows with these damned public service unions. Greedy, irrational and finally violent, but they control our politicians and no one is willing to take a tough stance with them.

Well, no sweat. Though I was hoping to make a big splash with these sample titles. Had journalist friends in the national press lined up.

Waiting for the thaw,

Bunty

From: Sandybeech@bloomsburynet.co.uk

To: BuntyB87@vsnl.com

Dear Bunty,

No sweat, stay where you are in Bombay. Isn't it called Mumbai now? You must explain when there's more time, but urgently now, I have packed and parcelled the same shipment to you by courier and only await the best address to send them to. Your enthusiasm is infectious. I told Petra and she said 'F...' the strike, send them by courier, regardless of the cost etc. So you have clout. And you must know good places to eat or club or hang out in Mumbai?

Ever,

Sandy

P.O. Tulsikazagam

District Pondicherry

Tamil Nadu

Dear Shyamalam,

This is written by courtesy of Mr K.N.L.T J. Subramaniam. First thing I asked him was why he had so many names and he was not replying but he said he is not going to act as censor. He is the community scribe so he will write in perfect English (He is BA also) whatever the client is wishing to convey.

Firstly, greetings from mother and loving younger sister Sitambari, who remembers you in prayers twice a day and is daily putting aside one ball of rice on her plate before she starts a meal just for 'brother who is away and will look after me always'.

Secondly, the rains have not come. The crop will not last but these are burdens beyond your control so do not be worried.

Thirdly, the boy's parents are willing to hold on for a little time, but then they have given notice that if no rupees reach them, they will be forced to look for another suitable match for their eligible boy and find some family with steady income.

This is becoming the word now in our caste. People are no longer looking for big riches. Just simply for a brother in the Gulf or in America. You must be regretting very much that you never did mathematics and becomes an engineer and applies for Green Card in America. That way marriage of your sister could be assured.

However, even nowadays that is not firm. You know the case of Mr Pillai, the postmaster's brother with that one son who went to America and after two months never sent another letter or any money. Just got happy by himself with some white woman. This is so terrible.

Now your news about younger brother Trippu, your Kakaji. There is no harm telling about his bad ways to me, his elder brother. I must to know what the rascal is doing. This is why his wife and son have left him and he is a widow. I told him long time to stop drinking and now he has drunk and his wife has gone, so he has drunk more. That is the vicious cycle.

You must pay no attention to it. God did not put it in the hands of nephews to save the fate of uncles. Let him rot and find another job and do not bother or worry that you are eating free or taking his advantage. Be assured, the Communist party will get him compensation from his employers forever. He has a very strong case. He must have tell you, one employer's son lifted his hand on him and beat him for being drunkard on the job. This is more of the same vicious cycle. He was drunken and beaten and dismissed and so he got drunken more. But his case is cast iron and the Communist leader here, with whom I have discussed very long this very case, says he is going to be comfortable because the owners don't want a court case and their son in jail for beating workers. The employing firm is getting American collaboration moneys and doesn't want any blushes or botheration.

Sitambari is saying that whatever fate and her family give to her, she will take it to her heart.

Hoping for good news,
Your good father,
Daddyji

From: BuntyB87@vsnl.com

To: Sandybeech@bloomsburynet.co.uk

Dear Sandy,

Will hang on in Bombay. Have fixed presentation. Bloody hot here.

Bunty

C734 Block 13

Lane No. 47, Workers Colony

Shivaji Link Road, Borivili

Bombay

Dear Daddyji,

I am afraid that news is still bad. I am going every day out after giving this no good for anything uncle cup of tea and making some idli in steam. I am waking five in the morning to catch early train for City.

Yesterday as I came out of the local station, just on main road a gentlemans stopping me. He said if I was employ and I say no. Then he tells that he is willing to give me a little job. My heart was delighted.

I walked a little space with him. He told he was a dentist person and fixing teeth good job. He called me up to his office with chairs and everything and explained me the problem. His dentist was in a gulley, very small alley and the entrance to his dentist shop was up on three stairs from very narrow doorway. He put up a very big sign saying tooth repairing and all this but nobody was coming because at the end of the filthy and narrow gulley on the main road there is two other big dentist who have come there long ago.

This gentlemans was very nice and he give me a thousand papers with his name and direction written on it and said to stand outside other dentists door and give it to customers and tell them it is much cheaper because of the small door in the gulley to have toothache and everything attended to by expert dentist.

I was giving hundred of this leaflet when the peoples from the Main road dentist come out and give me very bad slap. They take my papers and tear them up and kick me in bad places, throw me down and saying they are going to call the police. The real old dentist even comes in the street in his white mask and start cursing from behind it. His men told me that if they see me the same street they will beat me too badly and cut my liver and heart out and eat it as kebab. They were too ferocious and beastly.

Now I can't go in that railway station. I have to get down before and walk three mile round every day because these fellows may be waiting for me like they were threatening.

This is the kind of city, but do not be unhappy, I am not too damaged and will try and recover and be employed soon. Giving salaams to mummyji and sister,

Your loving and disappointing son,
Shyamalam

From: Sandybeech@bloomsburynet.co.uk
To: BuntyB87@vsnl.com

Dear Bunty,

Hope you got the consignment. How'd it go? Not the postal strike, the presentation! But maybe you haven't done it yet.

Bloody cold here. Wish I was there. Could soak up some of that Mumbai heat – what's a girl like me doing in a place like this?

Sandy

From: BuntyB87@vsnl.com
To: Sandybeech@bloomsburynet.co.uk

Sandy,

Wish you were here too, could show you around and you could help with the presentation, run the computer and dazzle them with a real authentic Brit presence – lower-middle-class Indians and the nouveau of Bombay are so racist, they lap it up. Waiting for the books. Cock up with courier not knowing the address and phoning my secretary. Have sent a personal car to their HQ.

Keep trucking,
Bunty

Just about to press the Send button when the bell rings and the books arrive. Thanks.

From: Sandybeech@bloomsburynet.co.uk
To: BuntyB87@vsnl.com

Bunty,

Glad they got there safe, good luck with the prezz.

What's to eat in Mumbai and what does one do in the evenings?

Don't get the wrong impression, I love exotic tastes but don't eat too much. I'm even relatively slim. There's an Indian restaurant round the corner which is great.

Official: Sending three fiction titles which Petra insists will go great in India. Kindly handle. Orders from above.

Ciao for Niao,
Sandy

From: BuntyB87@vsnl.com
To: Sandybeech@bloomsburynet.co.uk

Sands,

Never accused you of being fat, only said I wasn't. And what Indian restaurants in London – muck served up by Bangladeshis who wouldn't eat that stuff themselves. The Bongos have a rather good cuisine – fish plus.

Talking of which, went with friend to Trishna, which is Bombay's most exotic downtown south Indian swish-fish-dish diner. Then drink at a club in the Taj. Kids were dancing but one gets old and wears the bottoms of one's trousers rolled.

Off to the prezz as you dub it,
Bunts

C734 Block 13

Lane No. 47, Workers Colony

Shivaji Link Road, Borivili

Bombay

Dear Daddyji,

Wonderful and best news. Thanks be to God. I will not hesitate in conveyance, except to give greetings to my devoted mother and to my little sister Sitambari for whom all this is happening by the grace of the Gods who have granted for her happiness.

Be proud and swell out your chest. I have found employment.

My excitement, sir, is overtaking. Daddyji, just please bless your son. I will have the cash to send in a week's time. Mr Desai pays within the week. Guaranteed. The other salesmen are singing the praises.

And you will be so proud. This is not sales of hairbrushes and cotton handkerchiefs like we see on the pavement in Pondicherry, this is intellectual business. You was always saying you are wanting I should work with books. Now I am doing. I am in book trade. I have been employed as a salesman for literature works. Of course I am carrying with me magazines and other kinds of printings with film-stars, some magazines with ladies for men to see, but mainly I am trafficking in books.

I am representative for Mr Desai who is extremely kind gentleman from very high family and with good knowledge of the whole world. He told me 'South Indians is most intelligent and they deserve to be with their degrees and everything in the book trade.' I am starting Sunday Daddyji. Trial Period before becoming 'Specialist'. Please go to temple and pray for me. Give the news to motherji and to my sweetest Sitambari, the flower of our family, with whom, God willing, we have to depart with happiness and sadness very soon.

Your loving and dutiful son,
Shyamalam

From: BuntyB87@vsnl.com
To: Sandybeech@bloomsburynet.co.uk

Sands,

The presentation went very well. Problem is that they all feel there is a limited readership for such books. They said technical books, you know, real anatomy textbooks, stuff on computers goes well, but we are not in that boring business.

The Bombay guys say the sales of fiction are very sluggish. Makes me want to shout. Don't tell Petra yet, let me pull a trick or two.

Anyway back to my own personal grind. Will stay in Bombay for two weeks and see how far I get. A secret ...

Buntonella

From: Sandybeech@bloomsburynet.co.uk
To: BuntyB87@vsnl.com

Buntooshka,

So what's the big secret? A girl? A boy? Go on kid, out of the closet.
Bated breath.

Sandinista

From: BuntyB87@vsnl.com
To: Sandybeech@bloomsburynet.co.uk

Sandinista,

No, not a girl, not a boy. Will wait to see what you look like. Out of the
closet? Oh well – it's a book. A children's collection of short stories.
Don't want to say much more. Cultivate the muse with silence and
all that.

Roald Buntingdon

C734 Block 13
Lane No. 47, Workers Colony
Shivaji Link Road, Borivili
Bombay

Dear Mummyji and Daddyji,

Here is enclosed in the money order from PO Borivili first pay. It is not too much. I am owing the food shop some money so I have kept that back as he is giving more credit now that I have certificate of employ. Hope you will be happy.

I am at present selling computer science books and how to become a best manager in a few steps. People aren't buying too much. It is very risky running inside and outside moving cars in Mumbai traffic which is careless. The peoples in the cars are being called 'punters' by Mr Desai and the ladies punters asked me why I am selling get rich books and am remaining poor. I just smile and show teeth. One little girl, must be eight years said why am I wearing dirty shirt. I was ashamed. Her father saw this and was buying one magazine called *Asian Babes* which is coming from the UK.

Will send further remittance. Uncle is begging me to spend on drinks persistently and I am feeling very small compassion and giving him few rupees for cheap stuff.

Please tell sister Sitambari how things are looking up with the grace of God and make her to feel that if good lucks have come to me plenty good lucks will shower upon her.

Your worshipful son,
Shyamalam

From: Sandybeech@bloomsburynet.co.uk
To: BuntyB87@vsnl.com

Bunty,

I knew it, I knew it, I knew it! A writer, an artist. Can I be so forward as to presume that we are mates and that you will send me the first short story or any work in progress as it happens? Please, please?

Everest,
Sandy

From: BuntyB87@vsnl.com
To: Sandybeech@bloomsburynet.co.uk

Sandy,

Reluctant though I am, you are in the trade and a friend and constructive beyond duty, so I am entrusting the first story by attachment herewith to you. If you think it's the best thing since Roald Dahl, then give it straight to Petra or one of the editors you trust. Otherwise send me some constructive crit and I can rework it or keep it in mind for the next story. Is it useful to get an agent? I feel a fool asking you all this – I've been in the game for eight years but now I'm on the other side of the fence, or outside the tent pissing in.

Read fast and react!
Bunty

From: Sandybeech@bloomsburynet.co.uk
To: BuntyB87@vsnl.com

Bunty,

Yes, the story is fascinating. I've given it to Petra and told her to read it today!
If we publish it, I want the first signed copy and I'll get a free trip to India on official sales work.

Sandy

From: BuntyB87@vsnl.com
To: Sandybeech@bloomsburynet.co.uk

Sandy,

No news? What's the hang up, hold up, snarl up?

Bunty

From: BuntyB87@vsnl.com
To: Sandybeech@bloomsburynet.co.uk

Sands,

What's going on, no word for three days??? If the story is crap, tell me.

Bunty

From: BuntyB87@vsnl.com

To: Sandybeech@bloomsburynet.co.uk

Sandy,

I am back in Delhi. I hope you are using the right e-mail address.

Yours sincerely,

Bunty

From: Sandybeech@bloomsburynet.co.uk

To: BuntyB87@vsnl.com

Dear Bunty,

Don't get any of this wrong, but Petra has returned your story and didn't say anything for a few days. I grabbed her after a meeting and put the question straight and she says, 'Yeah, Bunty's story. I like it, but I don't think there's a market for that kind of fantasy about India. I think things have moved on and people want real books about India, the poverty, the caste system, the displacement of people by dams.' I didn't know what to say to her, so I am just passing on her remarks. This is not the only publishing house, you know. I really liked the old idea of the rope trick with the new twist of it being a rope that came back through the warp of space and was really a loop. Great idea. Reminds me of Jorge Luis Borges. What's the next one about? Is it about kids displaced by dams or having their kidneys stolen for transplants?

Sorry, but I am only an admiring middle-girl.

Yours ever,

Sandy

From: BuntyB87@vsnl.com

To: Sandybeech@bloomsburynet.co.uk

Sands,

OK, I can take that, but let me tell you something. Those three effing titles that Petra thought would go down so beautifully in India bombed. My reps couldn't shift even ten of them and the journalist I approached for a free and influential plug in the best mag in town, phoned me and said she got bored. So much for Petra's judgement.

Please don't misunderstand. I am not discouraged. No, my next story is not about hungry kids and the evils of genetically modified rice which fills people's stomachs, it's about a magic monkey man. I'll send it to you.

Later will be greater

Bunty

From: BuntyB87@vsnl.com

Dear Petra,

This may come as a surprise but Sandy reported back to me the remarks that you made about my short story. Yes, I did ask her to give it to you with a view to getting some encouragement. I think I know the Indian market better than you and can I say that India is right for the kind of thing I am writing.

And just by the way, your casual suggestion for the three titles you sent through Sandy didn't quite work. I regret to say that I wouldn't have chosen them as leading titles in the first place, but as you'll find, they are not going to make the firm any money in India – I could have told you that if you'd stuck to the terms of our contract and left me my editorial discretion.

Thank you for taking the time to read my story.

Yours sincerely,

Dilip Dilawar Singh
Director, Asia

C734 Block 13
Lane No. 47, Workers Colony
Shivaji Link Road, Borivili
Bombay

Dear Daddyji,

Mr Desai is doing wonderful benefits to us. He gives commission at the end of the very day. My one good friend on the sales representative force is called Kulwant Singh. He is a mad fellow and enjoys a lot. He is even trying to make me spend money in wicked places, but I am saving it and not going, even when he is saying he will pay. Mr Desai has made him Specialist in Motor car books. He has all car-wallah magazines called AUTO, AUTOMOBILE, WHEELS, BIKE WORLD, all such things and when he goes out, because he is a Singh, they trust him and place orders for the magazines.

Sometimes he can take away five hundred rupees.

Mr Desai is very expert at these specialities. He is training us to look for the right person for buying the right book. One other sales staff is a fellow with bulging eyes and flowing hair who looks like a madman and his speciality is Shobha De who is writing books with some naughty parts. This fellow, Bhyankar, can spot everybody who would like such books and he approaches them shamelessly, and turns the pages and even read little pieces. The college boys and lonely but rich old womans buy from him.

The secret Mr Desai tells, is to spot your customer. There is another fellow here called Shodhan. I think is from Gujerat. He is very sleepy fellow but with thick spectacles like an old medicine bottle. He is given the speciality of every books by Salman Rushdie. You must have seen about the book by this person in the newspapers about Muslim god. It is ban, but we are still making it available. Shodhan never say anything and his face is too serious. He can't do begging or show that he is pleased or sad or anything. Mr Desai has choosed him for these books and he is right. Shodhan is spotting all depressed persons like himself and selling Salman Rushdie books with no word spoken, just money passing.

Desai sahib is checking me every day. I am going out with general tasks with different titles. Soon he will be spotting my speciality.

I am too busy from morning to night. Kakaji is happy for me having job and is trying from the starting pistol go, to borrow cash for buying 'booj' is what he is calling saying this is English good word. I don't give him nothing, daddyji. I get plenty abuse and he try and lock me out at night and do black mails, but I push past the bugger, smashing the doors and then he start to cry but I don't care. I just sleep and go out to Mr Desai business next day.

This second big pay is coming to you dear Daddyji to do as you please inside this very envelope.

Please give my salaams to mummyji and my little sister. At last she will be relieved that her family is doing our duty and she can get happiness.

Your loving son,
Shyamalam

From: Sandybeech@bloomsburynet.co.uk
To: BuntyB87@vsnl.com

Bunty darling,

Have you gone stark raving marbleless? Writing angry notes to Petra?
Do you know who or what she is? She stormed into my office and
waved it in my face. She was furious. You don't do that to her. She
says you should get on with selling rather than trying to write – and
then she was less than complimentary. I tried to calm her down but
she was on the verge of picking up the phone and sacking you. Is
that what you want?

Yours,
Actually,
Sandy

From: BuntyB87@vsnl.com
To: Sandybeech@bloomsburynet.co.uk

Sands,

Sorry, it was hasty but I was hurt and furious etc. Fuck the bitch. But
of course I don't want to be sacked. What to do?

Bunty

From: Sandybeech@bloomsburynet.co.uk
To: BuntyB87@vsnl.com

Bunty,

Get successful. I have a small plan. There's a book here which is going ab fab. Hot cakeroons.

I mean publishing history, baby. I am sending it to you. Tell me what you think immediately.

Love,
Sandy

From: BuntyB87@vsnl.com
To: Sandybeech@bloomsburynet.co.uk

Sandrogynous,

Yes. I like it. And it's bloody fantasy, isn't it? I skimmed it but here's the marketing plan attached. OK?

I know we can pull this off,
Love,
Bunty

---

186 ADULTERY AND OTHER STORIES

From: Sandybeech@bloomsburynet.co.uk
To: BuntyB87@vsnl.com

Dear Dilip,

Thank you for your enclosure of yesterday.

Your marketing plan looks fabulous, though I feel confident, having received feedback from other English-speaking territories that the book and indeed the series can break cultural and class barriers and so urge you to consider a wider target audience. Expand by one ring, so to speak.

The product has made the concept of 'reading age' obsolete, relegated to the dustbin, a relic of late twentieth-century prejudice.

We sanction the shipment and the immediate strategy you propose.

Luck with the launch. With you in spirit. I believe your publication parties go on for three days and end in divorces all round the subcontinent – as my Brooklyn aunt would say, 'enjoy!'

Ever,
Sandy
(sales honcho?)

From: BuntyB87@vsnl.com
To: Sandybeech@bloomsburynet.co.uk

Hey Sandy memsahib,

Now I've actually doubled myself up in bed and read the book. It's pretty old-fashioned stuff. Not your Will Self – much more *Water Babies* – yeah, so you're going to say Water who?? You Englishers, even in publishing, are so badly read – check the Internet: Charles Kingsley dot com. Bound to be some dope.

But. Here's the great 'but', buddy boy/girl. Indians don't know England except as exactly THAT. They will read the book and immediately think this is for real. There are old farts in the Delhi Gymkhana who still think that P.G. Wodehouse is true! So magic, public schools with houses and bullies, wimps making good, Enid Blyton blushing in the wings – give it to the Indians, this is a winner!

Mademoiselle Rowling will be rolling in rupees. Is she single, or even if she isn't, does she want an Indian gigo?

Campaign blooms,
Bunty

From: BuntySingh999@hotmail.com
To: Sandybeech@bloomsburynet.co.uk

Sands,

Screw the Indian networks man, they are probably on strike. Haven't been able to access my mail for three days! Just go through hotmail, yeah? Your Potter, as I predicted, is first rate and the bookshops placed some heavy orders in the second week, but it's tailing off now. I don't know what the problem is, but we've had cancelled orders from six hundred 'stations' – that's jargon for agents here. Will check. Still, as John Donne would say, 'Do not ask for whom the till rings, it rings for Bloomsbury'.

nuff respeck'

(I heard that on BBC World, a serviceable phrase)

Bunty

From: Sandybeech@bloomsburynet.co.uk

To: BuntySingh999@hotmail.com

Bunty dear,

Dream on. From the great remove of London I know what the fuck has happened to your market. Bootleg. I've seen copies brought in by a writer who shall be nameless, but is very famous for glittering baubles – he gave us a copy of the fucking pirate edition!

What is it with India? I kidded myself that it was at least a pomegranate republic, you know, some style. But banana is the word! And that too rotting and bent.

Can anything be done, dear boy. The Honcho of International Marketing will be held by the balls with the holder's palm slowly turning, if we can't move on this. Go go go.

Sandy

From: BuntyB333@compuseve.com
To: Sandybeech@bloomsburynet.co.uk

Sands,

Yes, there is a copyright law. But the bootleggers rely on the fact that the courts take thirty years to get past the second line of a charge sheet. Bribery and corruption.

But, as always. 'Bunty is willin'. Here's the opportunity and the POA. This is serious.

Since HP is a universally known character and the book has made huge runnings (more BBC World tutelage), the government's junior Trade Minister who was with me in Delhi Public and then in college and is a friend, can be prevailed upon to make it a test case, set a trap.

Brace yourself. India hits the copyright barrier at a gallop.

And of course you must apply to come to India when the case comes to court and we can go to Goa for beaches or up to the mountains for dazzling scenery.

Want to meet you in person desperately.

In the saddle,
Bunty

P.O. Tulsikazagam
District Pondicherry
Tamil Nadu

Dear Shyamalam,

Mother and I are very grateful for the remuneration sent through post. However, since crop has failed we are using this sums for living on. Please remit more when possible for your circumstances. You too have to eat, my dear boy. Your sister is sad because money cannot go into dowry fund and her boy's people is getting impatient and rude. Calling names.

But please do not worry and if that bastard my younger brother gives you trouble, throw him out of his own house and throw his bottles after his person. Swine fellow.

Please replying soon,

Daddyji

C734 Block 13

Lane No. 47, Workers Colony,

Shivaji Link Road, Borivili

Bombay

Dear Daddyji,

The great news is that I cannot send you money by this envelope. Before you despair please read on. There is too much money and I am afraid to send it by this envelope so I am sending money order to your district Post Office which can be collected by you in person by supplying signature. And anyway those fellows at the Post are knowing you – I think it Pillai's brother-in-law? This time the money is double and triple the money I have sent last time.

This is all because of good Mr Desai and good fortune. When I reported for work he came down and tell me, 'Shyamalam, you are looking so innocent. Your face is showing wonder at every move of human people. Your smile is hypnotizing the children and their mothers. You are looking like you know everything and can be hurt by everything. I have finally found out your SPECIALITY. You are going to sell Harry Potter.'

From that day Daddyji, I was just going through every traffic at every street corner in Bombay where cars was stopping for half minutes or more and showing everybody in the vehicles my Potter. If the persons is having educated face or with children with tie or skirt or something like that, they are even calling me and purchasing books from my bag. I was saying the price and showing the covers with good pictures of fireful animals and English boy, and knocking at the car windows.

Daddyji, these peoples were miracle buying. I was picking up all the tricks. In some cars, I approach the back window and knock for the children sitting in back seat. Show them the cover. I say 'Harry Potter, Harry Potter' and the children who are seeing it on TV so they tell mummy or daddy and I say 'Cut price, cut price' and they roll the window and throw rupees. Sometimes I say 'Most selling with American childrens'.

On the fifth day, Sunday, I sold every copy I was holding by twelve o'clock in lunchtime. I went back running to Mr Desai's office for more and he got too excited too. We got into his car and he took me to Parel to his factory where the books is being made.

He said he would give me fifty boxes and to take them and store them in a flat which he has on hire for his girlfriend in Colaba and from there I could take every bagful every one hour and sell how much I like.

The printing press was making beautiful books. Colour covers coming out *phutta phutt* from the press, pages coming and cutting like karate chops, everything turned and stamp and sticking up. The ink was drying on pages, bright like rain on leaves. The smell was so romantic, like fresh breezes over the Bay of Bengal. Shobha De, Salman Rushdie, Sydney Sheldon, Stephen King, Harry Potterji, every good books.

Mr Desai took me personally to the flat and his boys put the boxes of books in the front room on the ground floor. Mr Desai's girlfriend, one fat, immoral person, came home and started some silly argument about not wanting to giving me any keys. She was telling that I may steal every of her things and run away and Mr Desai was protesting I was a good boy. Still she was looking at me as if I was a thief or maybe she was wanting to eat me, and I was looking at her knowing she is a loose girl and this she was seeing clearly so she didn't want me coming to her house. But Mr Desai is very profit minded. He was persuading her like anything and promising her electronics and new mobile phone. Mr Desai said he is soon finding more specialists for these same books and I can take charge of them, become a small boss myself. Harry Potterwalla with all titles of the same boy.

Every two days more books boxes had to be brought to the flat because they were selling very nice in the South Bombay. And then I went North Bombay where people are more buying Kulwant's motor car books but even here, standing with Kulwant I was selling out and going back for replenishments. Potterji, whatever it is, is magic stuff daddyji. When mummyji goes for prayers to temple tell her to ring one bell for him.

And please tell sister, her marriage is now a surety thing.

Your loving son,
Shyamalam

From: BuntyB@hotmail.com
To: Sandybeech@bloomsburynet.co.uk

Sands dear,

Yes, the ministry will cooperate. If we nip this bootleg in the bud, it will set precedents for copyright etc. That's the argument and the present govt. of India is going for it. So a detachment of cops has been detailed and all systems go. You have to make sure that when the trap is sprung the Brit papers give the fact of the government crackdown some prime space. Harry Potter, British interests – no excuse for not running it on the front page even in the *Daily Mail!* – Wog phobia balanced out – nasty wog bootleggers, valiant wog Minister of Trade!

Love you and leave you, but only till I hear,
XX
Bunty

From: Sandybeech@bloomsburynet.co.uk
To: BuntyB@hotmail.com

Bunting,

You persist in a very crude idea of British racism. It is much more subtle. It loves Indians. You are our children. Your woes are greater than ours, but like good parents our capacities, compassion and understanding of your crooked ways are only there to be at your service. Any chance our trade minister pal will accept help from Inspector Knacker of the Yard? The MD can arrange through connections with our ruling mafia. That way the Mail *will* big it up.

Like you, love you,
Sandinista

From: BuntyB@hotmail.com
To: Sandybeech@bloomsburynet.co.uk

Sandissimo,

Knacker? No chance. Indianization of law and order. This isn't some
Caribbean island, you know. The dragnet, even now, closes on the
wrongdoers. As the Mahatma said, 'If the cops are Indian, the bribes
stay within our borders.'

One fell swoop planned,
Buntode

C734 Block 13
Lane No. 47, Workers Colony
Shivaji Link Road, Borivili
Bombay

Dear Brother,

I am more worried than you will be. But I had to inform you. Our
boy Shyamalan has not reported home or slept here for ten days now.
I have informed police and am begging you now to send details of
any employment he may have obtained, as I am not knowing the
address or whereabouts or even nature of the same. He has left cloth
bags full of some non-study books which are all the same from which
I feel he is not reading them all but hawking copies.
Please don't be worried. I am doing my best.

Your brother,
Trippu

Mumbai Central Jail
Lower Parel
Mumbai

Ref: Prisoner No: GP 382732

Dear Daddyji,

I am begging you not to be panic when you see this envelope and letter and not to allow Mummyji to faint and not to even give whiff of these fallen circumstances to my younger sister Sitambari until I have overcome the present troubles.

Daddyji, they have swept down on me as I was selling my books on Kemps' Corner just under the flyover where there is always delays and traffic jam. It is the best place because lot of peoples is having children who are watching TV and going school and demanding Harry Potter. Day after day I was prospering there. You must have received my third and fourth money order. The police wallahs showed no mercy. They have kicked and beaten me in the back, face, front, side and in private parts. Requiring confessions.

I was telling them that I am a sales representative only and they say this is illegal and that what I am doing is against poor ladies in Britains who are writing and selling these books. Then I understand that I must never give Mr Desai's name because I have eaten the man's salt and will not send the police to him.

But this is knowledge they want. They say government is wanting to know. They beat me twice a day with ropes and tie me to the chair and ask me who is it giving me these book and who is printing them and where?

I have given them no answer. I will take their beatings, but I cannot talk about Mr Desai. When the police let me go he might even still give me another job.

I am sorry dear father, I cannot send any more money for time being but, god willing, Mr Desai will get me out of this because in pursuit of his business he got me into it. I cannot tell you more because they only give one paper for letters.

Your dutiful son,
Shyamalam

P.O. Tulsikazagam
District Pondicherry
Tamil Nadu

Dear Shyamalam,

Your father is too ashamed to write to you so I have got the pundit to put pen to paper for me. My darling son, why are you in jail? What have you done wrong? What sin? What murder? Your father tried to explain about some books and says they was about some magic in the books. Has the magic destroyed you? Is someone putting evil eye or spell on you? I should have told you never to deal with magic things, it could all turn against you. Remember that old woman Damyawati who used to put curse on other people's mango trees and what happened to her? All the mangoes on her own tree became birds heads and ate each other up. But my son, if you say you were simply, honestly selling why are they catching you in jail and bring such shame on the family?

We stay at home every day now. People will finds out and your father thinks there will be disgrace. Some nights he is saying that we must tie our bundles and leave the village before peoples is knowing that our son is in jail for Potter. How much sorrow you have brought on us with this Potter.

Your sister can now never be married in our district. Soon her boy's peoples is coming to know and then no one will want the sister of jail-going person. No money can help now. We are withdrawing from the boy's family the request for his marriage. Your father say we have no choice. Sitambari is crying like anything. Everyday she is crying. She is crying for you, not for her fate. Your father telled her that you were being beaten badly in jail like you wrote and he say it is good that you are being punished for selling Potter, whatever it is. She too is wanting now to leave this district and go somewhere where the disgrace is not known.

Pundit has to go to prayer now and he is writing this, so letter is finished. My dear son I will ring a bell for you.

Your mother,
Amma

Mumbai Central Jail
Lower Parel
Mumbai

Ref: Prisoner No: GP 382732

Dear Daddyji and Mummyji,

I still call you this because it breaks my heart that you no longer want me as your son. I can ask no forgiveness. Even to police and government I have confessed. I have sold Potter.

Four days ago the police told me that they had informed the Tamil Nadu police and that they were going to search your house for more books. I told that you people had nothing to do with my sins. I alone was guilty. Then they had found out that my younger sister's name was Sitambari and that she's trying for marriage in the district and they started making dirty remarks. I hit one of the police and threw myself upon him and bit his cheek. I tasted his blood, the bastard fellow. But then they have beaten me so I can't see from both my eyes clearly, just little bit through swelling.

I am the mud beneath your feet. I have betrayed you, my sister, and now, when I could not stand the beating any longer and they were sitting with my hands under the legs of a chair, I told them I would take them to the flat where the books were stored.

I had no other way of saving you. Or my hands. They said the police in our district would rape my sister and my mother. I took them to the flat where Desai's girlfriend stayed but there was no one there. The flat had been emptied out. Not one thing was left inside. No girlfriend, and she took her furniture and the book boxes.

The police then twisted me and said I was showing them wrong places. I had to take them to the printing press. Again we reached the place in the gulley where I knew it was and showed them the factory. It was silent and dark. When we went inside there was nothing there, just rats. No machinery, no printing, no people, no paper, no books, no anything.

They had gone.

The police didn't believe me. They said I had taken them to known empty places. But now they didn't beat me. They just threw me back in the jail and the senior policemen came.

They are taking me out of jail now and will bring me in court for this wrongs that I have done.

A big policeman came to me and said that Mr Desai and his girlfriend were happy and rich. They will never be caught because they give bribes. He is telling that I am the main culprit person, the Harry Potter Specialist and the British government and all big writers have spoken against me in a conference where peoples came from all over the world to talk only about scum people like me. Lock up for many years.

This is my fate.

I am begging you, even though you are not wanting me as your son, to forgive me. I was stealing nothing, giving the money properly back and Desai himself was giving commission. But the policeman is telling I should not have touched the Potter and become Specialist.

You will forget about me and so will my sister of yesterday, Sitambari, on whom I have brought shame and whose life I have brought into unhappiness. I will never forget you.

Your son of the past,

Shyamalam

From: BuntyB@hotmail.com

To: Sandybeech@bloomsburynet.co.uk

Sando,

We whacked them baby. They are on the run, their cohorts have been rounded up and the entire copyright pirating mafia in India is in a blue funk. Cops say they will get confessions, as Malcolm X would say, 'by any means necessary'.

Sales of the legit titles are up by six hundred per cent. God's in his internet haven and all's well with the web. Overseas sales department one, bootleggers nil.

Now plans to meet? In Inja's sunny clime where you should be spending time?

Kiss kiss,

Buntissimo

FIVE

say cheese

Mr Balkar was getting on, approaching seventy when he was almost persuaded to switch trades. Everyone in Poona knew him as 'Cent per Cent Balkar'. It was his boast, emblazoned on the permanent painted board which hung outside his house which doubled as his 'Academy', that every year he had a hundred pupils and that each one of them inevitably passed the exams. He would hold up his hand and say that's all he could or wanted to manage. He made great play of refusing anyone who turned up wanting to be the hundred and first.

There was no publicly verifiable tally of pupils, because apart from the sixty or seventy, who came to the five or six daily shifts at the Academy, he had several richer pupils whom he visited in their homes, charging them a great deal more than he did the class pupils. He claimed he kept this tally in a long register which he called the 'banya book' in which he wrote the boys' names – they were inevitably boys – and a note of the receipt of their monthly or weekly fee. The poor were required to pay weekly, the rich at the end of the month or whenever they chose.

'Cent per Cent' was a thin man. The flab on his neck gathered in wrinkles. His eyes were, in his sixtieth decade, none too good, but he didn't wear glasses. They were light green in colour, like those of a cat and were now narrowed to assist his failing vision. When looking at the exercise book of a pupil, he would scoop it up and hold it three inches from his face and move it up and down, professing himself satisfied or acutely unhappy with the way the particular sum in the calculus, in solid geometry, coordinate geometry, mechanics, statistics or one of the other mathematical arts, had been solved.

'This is a very good solution,' he would say, 'but unfortunately it is bloody wrong.' And he would put the book down on the table, at which ten pupils sat, and thump the offender on the back. It was never a really injurious blow, but just hard enough to cause a pause in breathing. His pupils were all between seventeen and twenty-one, far too old to beat. But there was the reminder of chastisement in his striking one of them on the back. He would then offer a suggestion as to the solution of the problem. Very often, he would pick out from memory an exam paper of some obscure university in some forgotten year, and indicate a similar problem and refer the pupil who was in error to it.

'Try Benares, June '38. Question 13 if I am not too mistaken.'

On the shelves at the back of the verandah, which had been converted into the Academy, open to the passer-by on the street to look into, because like a stage it lacked a fourth wall, there were classified stacks of these exam papers in little booklets. These were Cent per Cent's prized possessions, his library.

'Do not abuse the treasure,' he would say if one of the booklets was left at a diagonal to the shelves or if the piles were not precisely aligned after a pupil had returned a borrowed booklet to it.

At seven, when his last class ended, he would take a select pile of these papers in his khaki satchel which he slung across his shoulder, diligently put bicycle clips on his always khaki trousers and ride his bicycle to the houses of his 'private' pupils. He would do the rounds from seven each night and return sometimes at one in the morning, a little oil lamp attached to his handlebar, lit and smoking. Apart from the clump of stragglers and night owls gathered at the corner by the illuminated doorways of the teashop, the streets would be deserted. The stalwarts of the community, some of them ex-pupils now turning their mathematical skills to the prediction of cotton figures and to computing the winners of horse races, would shout their goodnights.

'Goodnight, sir' or 'Salaam, Professor Sahib.'

He would return the greeting with one finger flicked vertically from his forehead, a gesture he prided himself on having picked up from a British military officer of the Raj who didn't wish to waste his breath on politeness to no-counts.

It may have been as a result of a small but unexpected disappointment or reverse that he even contemplated switching trades.

Cent per Cent Balkar didn't have a phone. Most of the neighbourhood used the telephone of the Sachapir Restaurant, the corner teashop. Some even received their incoming calls there and the Irani proprietor would send a runner down to fetch the wanted person from his or her home and charge a small predetermined fee for the service with no sense of chagrin. It was part of his business and a matter of pride that apart from the doctor at the corner, the bicycle-renting shop and the rival restaurant opposite, his was the only phone in the neighbourhood and the only one which was open to the public for business. Sometimes an absent pupil who wanted a home visit from Cent per Cent would phone and have the request relayed.

'These nonsense boys,' he would say on receiving the message. 'The mountain is being called to Mohammad again. Only Mohammad will be charged double fees on judgement day. Yes. Now what nonsense problem have we reached here? Oho, oho, oho "asymptotes", very long word, very good puzzle.'

Early in this last academic year, when his fortunes changed, before he nearly threw his pupils to the mercy of the mathematics exam-paper-setters of Poona, a car drove up to his humble Academy. Cars of this make and polish didn't stop in that street every day of the week, so it drew a crowd of curious urchins and feckless passers-by. It was an English car, a very recent model, large and green, driven by a liveried chauffeur. A grand dame in a saree sat in the back, accompanied by a fat boy of seventeen whom the whole town knew as Mickey Gunwalla.

The grand dame was his aunt, the sister of his father. She was a Miss Moti Gunwalla, also well known in certain circles in town. She alighted from the car when the chauffeur opened the door. Activity at the blackboard and in the calculating minds of the problem-solvers at the table, came to a halt. She was coming up the steps of the verandah and proceeding to address Mr Balkar.

'You must be Mr Cent per Cent? Forgive me if that's rude, but my Mickey's friends tell me that you like to be called that,' she said, extending her hand and presuming he knew who she was.

'I do, madam, it is my work and my pride and joy.'

'And none of your pupils ever fail the examinations?'

'No madam, I am thorough with them. And strict. If they are likely to fail, ten days before the exam I encourage them to commit suicide, jump in the river and spare themselves, their families and myself the disgrace.'

'And do they take your advice?'

'I have had good results so far,' Balkar said. He invited her to sit on a stool vacated by a gallant lad nearest the blackboard, but Miss Gunwalla took in the offer and declined the seat. She had an enormous bottom and the stools in the tuition class had very minimal, potentially uncomfortable diameters.

'I believe you undertake tuitions,' Miss Gunwalla said, in the commanding cadence she used for questions.

'Yes, you can join one of my classes,' said Cent per Cent. He was aware that his boys were listening and he was elated that one of the known millionairesses of the town had condescended personally to ask for his assistance, but he was damned if he was going to show any grovelling gratitude for it. He wouldn't be rude or standoffish, but he could allow himself this little game of pretending not to quite understand.

'It isn't for me, Cent per Cent,' said Miss Gunwalla. 'It's our boy Mickey, you know, he goes to Wadia College, but there's such a rowdy atmosphere in his class, with boys and girls being rude to the professors and throwing paper darts, that the poor fellow is confused and getting his sums all wrong. I have been to the college and tried to tell them that he has a delicate temperament, but they are not interested. Soon we'll send him to France to a private tutor, or England but his father has got it into his head that he must "rough it out" and pass these exams here first. Poor fellow. Can't you help him?'

'There are no cat-calls, paper darts, brickbats and so on in my lessons, here,' said Balkar, proudly indicating his pupils who dutifully pretended to get back to their problem-solving, flicking through the pamphlets of the past papers and scribbling diligently.

'I am not sending him here,' Miss Gunwalla said. 'He has allergic reactions to certain places. It's very comfortable at home. We'll find you a good place in the library where he normally does his homework. If six o'clock three times a week would suit you?'

Cent per Cent held up his hand.

'I must examine the pupil first before accepting anything.'

'We can send the car to pick you up every day.'

'My dear Miss Gunwalla, I have been cycling to tuitions for forty-five years now and am not going to change the habits of the old dog. And my classes extend till seven, so earliest I can come is seven thirty.'

'But he plays the mandolin at seven thirty,' said Miss Gunwalla. 'Look Cent per Cent. What are we talking about? Your fifteen pupils in two classes? I can pay you more than all thirty of them put together.'

Miss Gunwalla thought this was the most logical solution to the problem and would be welcomed on all sides. It had an electrifying effect on the pupils who looked at each other. One or two smiled. This lady was serious.

'They can shift their times till later,' she said. 'After you finish at our house.'

Everyone waited for Cent per Cent's reaction to the offer.

He drew his wrinkly neck up like a snake under the spell of a charmer's nasal flute.

'I eat my dinner between five fifty-five and six o'clock. It is the habit of my childhood.'

'I am sure we can come to some arrangement. I am here Mr Cent per Cent because everyone in town tells me you are the best.'

She had struck Cent per Cent in his Achilles' heel. His resistance to professional flattery was very low.

'I will come and see you tonight,' he said and added, 'If you will be so kind as to give me the address.'

Miss Gunwalla and the pupils knew very well that Mr Balkar was pulling a fast one. He knew that the Gunwalla mansion was one of the sights of Poona. It was called 'Canons' and sported four heavily chained cannons on gun carriages, cast, as their plaques proclaimed, in the forges of the Gunwalla factories in Gujarat on a commission for the navies of the East India Company. Through successive generations, the family had supplied arms and ammunition to the British Raj and the scions of their clan had, in gratitude, been given Baronetcies and been knighted.

Still, Miss Gunwalla took him at his word and offered to write the address down for him and did it standing up, writing merely the name of the house and 'Poona Camp' under it.

'You can ask any policeman,' was her retort to his little show of arrogance.

The car parted the crowd of gathered, gaping urchins, and left the street.

'You see these nonsense people,' said Cent per Cent when she had gone.

'They think they can buy my class out. Never, you heard me. Never, I said. I would rather lose the ten fingers on which I do calculations, to leprosy, than change my pupils' times to suit the rich.' He had convinced himself that that was the retort he had produced in refusing her offer.

'No you didn't, sir,' said Doongar, one of the stalwarts of his class. 'You were scared of her. You muttered something about having your meals, sir.'

'You better clean your ears out Doongar; you are hearing very wrong things,' said Cent per Cent, holding Doongar's book up to his face to check how far he had progressed with the problem in hand. 'And you should give up mathematics and take up playing the dholak in the street and rent yourself out for festivals. Make assets for your family who suffer your existence.'

Doongar was used to it. He grinned at the rest. They and Cent per Cent knew that the master was duly ashamed of his deference to the authority of wealth.

But he couldn't contain his excitement at the offer and straight after his last class he pedalled to Canons. There was a chowkidar at the gate and a dog who had to be restrained while Mr Balkar was admitted.

The house itself was an old colonial mansion with some pretensions: Doric columns to frame the porch, a fountain with a statue of Neptune riding a shoal of dolphins and a coat of arms in plaster of Paris on either side of a door whose wood, Cent per Cent learnt later, had been specially imported from Norway all those years ago by a grateful English admiral who had won a few sea battles using their family-made guns.

A maid opened this door and looked Cent per Cent over, leaving him standing in the large circular hallway with a big carved table in the centre, a bowl of goldfish on it and a chandelier hanging above it.

The Gunwallas had very eclectic taste.

Miss Gunwalla was gushing and grateful and sat Mr B down and was now willing to compromise on the time of the lessons. She suggested mornings, and said he should start at seven. Cent per Cent's expressed wish to see his pupil and test his adequacy was again brushed aside. The boy was being given an oil massage and would then be served his dinner. This was no time for tests. The fee that Miss Gunwalla offered was considerably less than what it would have cost to buy out two of his evening classes but still, it was a good twenty times what he charged the poor boys of the town who came to him to enhance the scores on their maths papers.

Cent per Cent was not so much a teacher as a problem solver. His stock in trade was repetition, taking these past examination papers and solving them so that the pupils could watch the unfolding of the logic, could divine a pattern in the problem-solving and even in the trick of problem setting. A peripheral conceit of his was, towards the day of the actual exams, to predict the problem that would be set in each category and class of maths and in each section of the paper, down to the last algebraic digit, though avoiding the actual numerals which, he said, even the guys who set the paper didn't know.

There was no scientific proof of his clairvoyance in this matter because once a paper had been completed, those who had done well wouldn't want to go over the territory of their triumph and those who felt they had done badly would try and forget it. Very few would take the trouble to compare what Cent per Cent had predicted with what actually appeared in the exam, but still his reputation for crystal-ball gazing and uncanny accuracy at this sport had spread, and was widely whispered year after year. A session or two at the Academy, before each university final, would be dedicated in reverent silence to an unveiling of the predictions for the next day's exam paper.

Tutoring Mickey Gunwalla did entail cancelling some other pupils' lessons but Mr Balkar told himself that these little readjustments were the fabric of life and at any rate two of the readjusted pupils whom he taught as a pair at seven in the morning were just giving themselves airs by being privately tutored. They could very well come to his evening class. Their parents were not rich or grand enough to command his exclusive attention. Not that Mr Balkar was a snob but he did believe that the enterprising got rich and the hardworking were rewarded in the end. His own circumstances, which clearly contradicted this principle, didn't seem to negate its persuasiveness.

He made it to Canons at seven o'clock on his bicycle. Miss Gunwalla had neglected to inform the watchman at the gate so Mr Balkar had to wait for at least twelve minutes, being sniffed and barked at by the ample female dog of the house, a sloppy, overfed Labrador by the name of Tooshka.

There was further delay as he was seated in a very large greenhouse at the side of the house at a table waiting for Mickey to wake up and present himself for the tutorial.

Miss Gunwalla eventually came in and Cent per Cent got to his feet. He had slung his satchel on the back of the chair and taken a few exam papers and a small slate and a stick of chalk which he carried, in lieu of a blackboard, and placed them on the table.

'You will have breakfast, Cent per Cent?' asked Miss Gunwalla.

'I have already eaten,' said Cent per Cent, lying. He had had a cup of tea at the corner cafe on the way.

'Nonsense,' said Miss Gunwalla and gestured to the servant who was already holding the tray with toast and coffee and an omelette concealed under a silver salver.

Mr Balkar ate as Miss Gunwalla watched. He wasn't allowed eggs at home. His wife was a strict vegetarian but her strictness didn't stretch this far into Poona high society. Mr Balkar would sneak off and eat a lamb biryani at the local Irani restaurant when he felt like it. One or more of his pupils would inevitably spot him, but he didn't mind. He was rather proud of being a modern Brahmin, one who had adapted to the changing times.

The great surprise of the breakfast was a cylinder of cheese with concentric rings on its surface, marks of the tin it had come in. Mr Balkar immediately knew what he was looking at.

This was better than the occasional eggs and biryanis. This was Kraft cheese.

He said as much to Miss Gunwalla who had watched him swallow the omelette with a mixture of pleasure at his appetite and disgust at the squelching, belching way he absorbed the lot. But the cheese. Ah, the cheese.

'Kraft! My father used to get it during the war. You don't see it much nowadays,' he said, as Miss Gunwalla cut him a segment from the circular slab.

'Smugglers,' said Miss Gunwalla. 'You can get it from Bombay smugglers.'

Cent per Cent didn't care that it was contraband. He relished the taste of 'real' cheese.

Every subsequent day he was given the same breakfast. It became a routine as Mickey became more punctual and as there was no delay at the gate and he wolfed it down. Some days it was Kraft cheese with biscuits, some days with toast. The only annoyance was Tooshka who never gave up snapping and barking at his heels and had to be led away each day, snarling and dissatisfied, seeming to wonder at the foolishness of the servants and the household for admitting this intruder.

Three times a week he would try and teach Mickey mathematics and muster from within fresh resources of patience as Mickey failed to grasp the very idea of differentiation and integration, no matter how many illustrations Cent per Cent gave him, and utterly failed to grasp how three numbers on axes could fix a point in space.

But the cheese kept coming.

The household must be in regular touch with these smugglers, thought Mr Balkar, but put the thought from his mind as not any part of his business. The service slackened as the weeks went on and sometimes the Kraft cheese would be simply served to him in its flat blue tin with segments of it already cut away by other eaters.

And then one day Miss Gunwalla announced that there was no more cheese. The household's stock was exhausted and the particular smugglers in Bombay with whom they were in touch, had been arrested and jailed. Other smugglers of Kraft cheese had taken fright from these events and gone underground. There hadn't been a blue tin on the black market for months. Not for love or money could you buy it, but Miss Gunwalla said she knew some people in the French embassy and she would ask them.

When, after some weeks, Mr Balkar diplomatically enquired as to the outcome of this contact with the French consular staff, Miss Gunwalla, who had been to Bombay and must have initiated some investigation into the cheese famine, was rather curt.

'They were very snobbish about it,' she said. 'That bloody Frenchman I asked said that he didn't know what Kraft cheese was and that in France any such thing wouldn't be recognized as cheese at all.'

This puzzled Cent per Cent. Surely Kraft was the king of all cheeses? Not that he knew of any other. The rebuff had disappointed and even annoyed Miss Gunwalla.

'His command of English was very poor,' she said.

'If we can't import it, we should make it,' said Mr Balkar and thus began the great adventure.

It was, at the time, a frivolous remark, but a few days later Miss Gunwalla raised the subject again.

'Do you really think we can make cheese here?' she asked.

'We make paneer, and that is a kind of cheese. My wife makes it every day.'

'That is cottage cheese, but I am thinking of making real cheese, like Kraft. Why not? It must be milk with something else.'

Something else. It was in quest of this something else that Mr Balkar cycled to his old college in the city. It had a library dating back to the college's foundation in the nineteenth century and he happened to know that no books had been removed from it since British days. The British were curious about everything. He would certainly find a book on the making of cheese.

And he did. He found a very old book called *Cheeses and their Moulds* by Henman Bargery.

This Bargery, as Cent per Cent discovered, was a botanist and had made a commendable study of the growth of the organisms, the moulds or fungi which interacted with the fats and acids of milk to transform it into the stuff that finally became cheese. Cent per cent was fascinated. He held the book to his face, ignoring the curious glances of the young pupils using the library and stayed there reading through the day. He phoned the cafe at his street corner to relay a message to one of his classes that he had been held up and would give them an extra lesson late that night.

Bargery's language was like nothing he had come across before.

He referred to cheese as a battlefield and a hive of activity, a living thing, a geography in miniature, a miraculous transformation into preservable nature. He talked of Greece and Rome and Ancient Britain, of the Arabs and of Babylon. He compared cheese to wine, its multifarious flavours and attractions and left Cent per Cent even more puzzled as he had never tasted any wine. It was another comestible about which Cent per Cent knew nothing.

'It cannot be popular in India,' Cent per Cent said, basking in the confidence of his new knowledge when next Miss Gunwalla revived the subject.

'And why is that?'

'Because the curd or soft gel is formed by the chief protein in milk which is casein, but then it has to be subjected to rennin which is an enzyme found in stomachs of young baby cows and has to be extracted by salting their intestines. How can you do that in India with all these Hindus who don't do cow slaughter? Finished.'

'Not at all finished,' said Miss Gunwalla. 'We don't have to tell them. What they don't know can't hurt them.'

There was an irrefutable logic to this, Mr Balkar had to admit.

He repeated the phrase to himself as he cycled at eight thirty into the waking hubbub of the city. What they do not know cannot harm them.

It was then that Miss Gunwalla took up the idea in earnest. A few days later she presented Mr Balkar with three books.

One was in French and she said she would have all of it translated, but the other two were hardbacks called *Fromages* and *Manna from Milk.*

'Read them. We will start small and go big,' Miss Gunwalla said.

And just as he had with Henman Bargery's great work, Mr Balkar entered into a whole new world.

'We need space and we need penicillium camemberti and penicillium rocqueforti and the bluish-green veins of penicillium glaucum.'

'I hope you know what you're talking about Cent per Cent,' said Miss Gunwalla.

Soon another outhouse was built, of glass and bent wrought iron with a skirting of brick and wood. It was something between a greenhouse and a factory and under Mr Balkar's direction, the beakers and test tubes and great barrels and churns for the milk and for curds and whey were bought and installed.

Mr Balkar spent all his spare time at Canons, ordering this and that from France and Britain and not via the mail either. It was to be brought in, smuggled at times by the relatives, friends and employees of the Gunwallas who travelled to these places or were induced to do so.

This work of setting up a cheese partnership with Miss Moti Gunwalla began to eat into his teaching time. Still, Cent per Cent tried to honour both commitments, the old and the excitingly new. He began to let the obligations of his old life slide. He was late for his classes. He hurried off as soon as the class was done. He spent a lot of the time in his classes reading books about cheese, holding them right up to his face as his range of four inches decreased to three and to two and a half.

The shed was soon completed. It had never been said and no paper had been signed, but the Gunwalla-Balkar partnership cheese industry, a pioneering step in the modernization of India, was all set to go on a fifty-fifty basis.

The most unpleasant duty Balkar had to perform was going to the Muslim abattoir in search of this rennin. The butchers in that stinking charnel house didn't know what he was talking about so he had to go through the process step by step. He wanted the intestines of young calves. That they understood. All sorts of perverts came to them and asked them for the strangest bits of animals. He would take them away, he said.

Miss Gunwalla asked him to supervise the two servants who were assigned to the task of extracting, over a boiling stove, the chemical from the slimy, grey, bloody and snotty mess of intestines he went back for each week. He had to then test the brine extract to check its concentration of rennin as the books told him to do.

Mr Balkar became a man possessed. He lived now by the disciplines of his new obsession whereas he had for forty years lived the year out by the date and advent of the exams, the start of the new term, the registration of pupils, the anxieties of the last months, the declaration of his Cent per Cent results and the distribution of sweets by his pupils who came to thank him for their passes.

Now he lived by thermometers and barometric readings in the greenhouse, by density measurements of milk, by the ceremonies he conducted, decanting the cultures of the moulds from their sealed metal containers to test tubes and trays in which they could breathe and grow. And all this to the constant and irritating barking of stupid Tooshka who still, after months, looked upon him as the enemy and howled her protest at his presence in the grounds.

The cheese was a disaster. The first container when it was opened was still a liquid mess. Miss Gunwalla insisted that he taste it. Mr Balkar felt sick. It was bitter and frightening. They threw it all away and cleaned the moulds and the milk containers and started again.

New cultures arrived from France and Britain and new books which talked of the setting up of cheese presses and waxing moulds.

And then for the first time in years, on the night when the university results were to be declared and the streets were alive with the sounds of expectant students and their families, Mr Balkar was on the verandah with a book about cheeses. He would normally be rubbing his hands, as anxious as a prima donna before her first appearance. But on this results day, it was as though the plague of exam fever had passed.

The students stood in the street outside and as the newspaper boys sped past with their piles of newspaper sheets on their handlebars screaming 'Rizzz-eee-o-ult', they grabbed the sheets and scoured them for their own exam numbers.

Yes, all of Mr Balkar's pupils had passed in the first class – all except one. Mickey had failed.

Mr Balkar stepped into the street. It was the first time any such thing had happened. He asked a student to check the number again on the result sheet. There was no number. The failures weren't on the list. He checked the third class passes. Mickey's number did not appear.

Mr Balkar, surrounded by jubilant and grateful students, looked at the board above his verandah. It said Cent per Cent results. That was no longer true. A pupil of his had failed the exams.

What was certain was that the Gunwallas weren't going to proclaim it and no one in the town needed to know. What they didn't know wouldn't hurt them, was the little devilish fish that swam round and round in Balkar's pond of bitter disappointment. He blamed himself, he blamed cheese. He blamed the genetic unteachability of the Gunwallas.

The other ninety-nine pupils came round to congratulate him and each other and he negligently forgot to buy the sweets that he would customarily and reciprocally distribute. He felt like a fraud. The advertisement outside his classes, the lifeline of his business as a tutor was now a lie. One sheep had strayed, one fellow-traveller had fallen by the wayside. On the other hand, what the world did not know wouldn't hurt the world. He would conceal his shame. He would not change his board: 'Ninety-nine per Cent Balkar.' It didn't have the same ring.

Miss Gunwalla said Mickey's pocket money would be cancelled and he'd be sent straight to Canada to his cousin's as a punishment.

She and Balkar had decided after their first disaster to reduce the scale of the operation. They would make a small quantity first. This second small quantity of cheese looked like cheese but didn't taste like it. It crumbled into a lumpy mess and it tasted sour and bitter and no amount of bread or biscuit would help it go down the gullet. Again they had to throw it away, readjust the temperatures and the humidity of the greenhouse by various desiccating devices and start again.

Miss Gunwalla suspected that Balkar was losing heart and kept urging him on with, 'Think of the profits, think of the monopoly we shall have, think of the riches throughout India when everyone will be selling and buying and eating our cheese at half a billion breakfast tables and in half a billion fridges ...'

Yes, Balkar could see this. Not the fridges and breakfasts in that precise quantity, but he could see their ultimately canned product gracing the tables of the rich. From the Karakoram and Kashmir to Kerala and Kanyakumari – oh yes, he knew his geography – 'Cent per Cent Cheese', perhaps?

Tutoring, the central activity of his life for forty years, was now becoming just a way of earning his money. Cent per Cent knew that the pupils had noticed this slide in attitude, but the preoccupation with his new books and tubes and cultures made it difficult to concentrate on the mundane matters of solid and coordinate geometry.

And his library on cheese now occupied a whole shelf above his bed, where books on maths and duplicate copies of the examination paper pamphlets had rested. Oh yes, there were books on the cheeses of France, on blue cheeses, on English cheeses, on new methods of curdling milk, on moulds, funguses and their patterns of growth.

The secret, Mr Balkar found, was in the milk and therefore in the herd of cows from which the milk was obtained and thence depended on the feed that the cows were given. He scoured the whole of the state, going to farmer's meetings, calling at dairies on his bicycle, speaking to the deputy of Bombay's largest milk 'colony', a cooperative of suppliers, to find where the richest milk was to be found.

The farm on which his choice finally alighted was a hundred miles from the town and he had to ask Miss Gunwalla in his most diplomatic manner for a specially cooled and stable truck to fetch in the churns over that distance.

He had spent a lot of his own money on the enterprise. Miss Gunwalla, being rich, had no regard for where other people got their money and seemed perfectly willing to let Cent per Cent spend his share. After all, it seemed to be understood that they were partners.

Cent per Cent didn't think of himself as living a lie. The next year's intake of pupils hadn't come in yet because the long summer holidays were on and the temperatures of April and May would necessitate coolers and air conditioners and humidifiers in the cheese factory. They were duly installed, though Miss Gunwalla made a song and dance of it, going over the cost of each piece of equipment ten times and writing it all in a book while insisting that Cent per Cent sit on a stool in the factory and listen to the litany of costs, while Tooshka barked her head off outside.

Miss Gunwalla muttered about the project not taking off and draining her patrimony. Cent per Cent was embarrassed, but on the outside remained stoic. He knew that to the Gunwalla family, a thousand cheese sheds and experiments would be but a drop in the ocean. For him it was so much more.

He had foregone his annual holiday for two weeks to the little
resort in the hills called Panchghani where he and his wife went
each year to the same guesthouse where they rented a room
and where his wife did much the same as she did at home in
Poona, which was going to the market and preparing the meals
on the kerosene stove. Only the evenings, after their meal, were
different. They would walk out in Panchghani to one of the hill
'points' – places from which one got a view of the valleys – and
they would return as dusk was gathering, to the little room in
the guesthouse and Mrs B would say prayers to the little idol
she carried with her and they'd extinguish the kerosene lamp
that lit the room and sleep before nine o'clock.

They had followed the same routine for each day of the
holiday and the same holiday for the last twenty-five years.
His wife said nothing when he announced the cancellation.
It was not her place to speak about such things or to object.
And so what if the holiday had been unexpectedly cancelled?
Being Mrs Balkar was privilege enough. Not that she didn't
notice that the sacrifice of the holiday was in aid of the cheese
business which he was carrying on with the rich Parsee lady
who lived in a big house in a part of town into which she had
never ventured. He said it was going to bring them fortune
and a new life, but she listened to him without indicating that
she had heard it, going about her daily chores and ceremonies
without tempting the gods with these dreams and avaricious
illusions and ambitions.

Eventually the day came when they got the conditions right
and the cheese was made. It was creamy with light veins of
mould showing and it had exactly the right moisture. Cent per

Cent opened the casing of the first container and couldn't stop staring at it. Then he timidly ventured to take a taste. Yes. It was the correct texture and for the first time that bitterness, the yeastiness, the nasty after-taste were absent. It was a good but runny cheese.

Cent per Cent was excited beyond measure. He opened the other casings and there they all were, mummified and soft in their wax. He had struck soft gold. He tasted another consignment and then another. They were the same.

He dashed to the main house shouting for Miss Moti.

It was early morning and she came rushing in her dressing gown with curlers in her hair and crossed over to the greenhouse, somewhat detached from the main mansion. Mr Balkar hadn't even taken his bicycle clips off.

'Close your eyes and open your mouth, Miss Moti,' he said, and using a palette put a bit of their glorious cheese on her tongue.

'It doesn't taste anything like cheese,' she said, opening her eyes.

'What do you mean?' He was astounded.

'It just doesn't taste and feel like cheese. You can eat it, but who wants to eat that?'

He could have screamed.

'It doesn't taste like Kraft cheese,' she explained.

'It's not Kraft cheese. This is a French culture. That's what we've been trying for the last year, madam.'

'A French cheese?'

'Just like they eat in France. That embassy person was right. This is much better. Kraft cheese is processed cheese. It's not cheese at all. It's plastic rubbish.'

'My family has eaten it for generations,' said Miss Gunwalla.

'Your family should have tasted Camembert and Roquefort and Stilton, Emmentaler and Gruyere from Switzerland and Edam from Holland.'

He would have gone on, but it seemed rude. Cent per Cent had never himself tasted any of these cheeses. But he had seen their pictures and read about the culture that made and surrounded them. He had never tasted Camembert, but he knew the taste by its literary description and he knew he had something like it here. Of course that's what he had. He had used the penicillium camemberti. At the time he'd sent for the cultures of moulds he had not known what the cheeses would turn out like, but he had learned to love the photographs of the cheese in their wax moulds, in their cut state on boards, in cross-section and on the tongues of afficionados.

'But I ordered you to make Kraft cheese,' said Miss Moti Gunwalla.

That hit Cent per Cent hard. 'Ordered?' he said.

'Yes, ordered. You have spent all my money on making some bad pudding, when I wanted cheese.'

Mr Balkar was stunned. They had reached the summit, like Hillary and Tenzing, together, and now she was saying she wanted to climb another mountain, that this was not the one.

'I think you know nothing about cheese,' he said.

'I think you have wasted my money, Mr Balkar, and if this is the best you can do, you had better go.'

'Go? Yes, I will go,' Balkar said 'And I will take my cheese factory with me.'

He didn't know what he was doing, but he went to the outhouse and as Miss Gunwalla watched, Mr Balkar fetched his bicycle and, emptying his khaki satchel of its books, filled it with test tubes and cultures and anything he could get his hands on. He took the vats of cheese and tied them together. He found a cardboard box in which the latest material had been delivered and threw equipment into it and strapped it onto the handlebar of his bicycle. Miss Gunwalla watched while he did all this and then she called for the servants and the chowkidar. Four men came running to the shed and they restrained Mr Balkar, took the packages and equipment off his bicycle and threw them carelessly all over the floor. The test tubes were smashed, the cultures spilt, the cheeses were chucked on the tabletops and left plopping on the floors.

'My cheese, my cheese,' Mr Balkar shouted, but at a hint from Miss Gunwalla, and with Tooshka barking her head off, the servants dragged him protesting to the gate. They threw him out and hurled his bicycle after him. Balkar and the bicycle landed in the gutter as the metal gates of Canons shut behind him and a servant restrained the dog who had finally triumphed in expelling the suspect intruder.

Mr Balkar cycled home down the slopes to where he lived. He didn't tell his wife what had happened. In his mind and on his lips was one mantra: 'Kraft is not real cheese.' This was funny because it was the only cheese he had ever eaten and still the taste and splendour of it lingered in his memory, but he had given the effort of the last year to something else, to cultures that had taken the Europeans centuries to perfect. Miss G could know nothing of that and wanted to know nothing of it.

The next day Mr Balkar cycled back to Canons. He had made up several lines in his head which he would use on Miss G, but on getting to the gates found that he was treated as a stranger. He was kept out. He decided to squat by the gates and when the postman came by, he challenged him to give him the parcels which were in his name. There were indeed letters addressed to him, but the postman was in a dilemma. The address was clearly Canons and Mr Balkar, whom he knew, was clearly being exempted from the property. The postman decided in favour of the de facto power and handed the parcels to the chowkidar who took them into the house.

'They contain new cultures,' said Balkar to the chowkidar and the other servants who came out to jeer at and pity him. 'No one but me will know what to do with them, you nonsense people.'

They paid him no attention. Miss Gunwalla didn't seem to be home. Mr Balkar came back the next day and the next. He spent the day waiting with his bicycle next to him outside the forbidding iron gates of Canons. On the third day he was there, a large car drew up, the gates were flung open and Mr Balkar saw that the car contained Miss Gunwalla and two white men. The gate closed behind them after the car entered.

The next day, drinking a cup of tea in the Sachapir restaurant, a headline in the Poona Herald caught his eye:

'French Embassy says Gunwalla Cheese is Real Native Stuff'

The article under the headline said that Miss Gunwalla had discovered the formula for the best cheese that India could grow. It had been accredited by the French themselves and a factory to produce this cheese in bulk was to be set up by the Gunwalla estate in collaboration with France.

He asked the restaurateur if he could use the phone and he tried to call Miss Gunwalla. The servants said she was not at home.

Of course he had been cheated. Now they would make their millions from the cheese he had researched and made. She didn't even like it, but then she didn't have to. The Gunwallas were not great fighters of sea battles and slaughter on the waves, but they had made their millions from guns whose muzzles poked out from the sides of ships. He phoned her again and again and finally he reached her. Miss Gunwalla was brief.

'I am sorry, Mr Balkar, I am a lady and I am not used to being spoken to in the terms you were using. Please never darken my doors again.'

'What about my money? My partnership?' Cent per Cent said, a frog in his throat.

'I know of no agreement with you. You came here to tutor my nephew Mickey and you did that very badly, so that he failed. If I hear any more from you, I will sue you for ruining a year of his life with your bad teaching.'

She put the phone down.

Cent per Cent sat on the empty verandah where his classes were held. No harm had been done. He could get a hundred pupils when term started. He was sure of that. He would, for his own conscience's sake, take down the board which said 'Cent per Cent' and just call himself, very modestly 'Balkar's Classes'. That was the truth.

He would book the Panchghani holiday and take his wife. He understood a little more, in his seventieth year, about life, people, fortune and the vanity of human wishes.

But did he?

The day after Mr Balkar had his notice board repainted and left for Panchghani on the State Transport Bus with his wife and baggage, Tooshka the dog, agitated by the mice and rats that had got into the cheese factory, apparently smashed through the glass of the greenhouse and ran amok. The test tubes and the cultures and cheeses were flung all about and smashed. Irreparable damage was done.

The next day Tooshka's eyes were filmed over with a green pus. Her golden coat of hair had flecks of black woolly stuff on it. She spread the fungus she was cultivating on her painful eyes and coat to the cats, to the carpets, to the curtains, walls, the felt of the billiard table, the kitchen, pantry and odd corners of the great house. The denizens of Canons, including Miss Gunwalla, the servants, the chowkidars, even one or two visitors were infected and developed sticky eyes and itchy skins on which patches of very many different colours appeared as the weeks wore on.

The great house was, on the advice of doctors, closed to visitors and tradesmen for weeks while experts were called in to defungify the people, the pets and the premises. There was no further news of the French collaboration.

In the year after these events, Amul, an Indian dairy manufacturer, began to market a cheese very close in texture and taste to the processed Kraft.

SIX

short stem judas

Friends, I'm sorry to address you. Or what I mean is, you must know, that you didn't come to hear me.

Some of you may have come to this session expecting to see Madhu Devdar of Rajasthan talking about the first-hand experience of his village with the agrarian products that Interseed Inc. have seduced, bribed, cajoled, blackmailed and cheated the villagers into buying. I apologize for my own appearance on this platform instead. I need to tell you exactly what's going on. You've seen the press release which we, the Round Table of Eden 2000, put out yesterday and you've probably read what the newspapers – crap – have put out today. And the BBC did this kind of edited, distorted interview with me this morning. Which I want to disown.

The facts are these, brothers and sisters: we had every reason to believe that Madhu had been kidnapped by persons unknown and taken away in the car that the police themselves said was a black Honda of W registration. He was seen in the company of two men who seemed to have him captive at a remote petrol station on a road in Dorset. Are the papers calling the police liars? A guy fiddling with the handle inside trying to get out? Yeah, they said the car was baby-locked and the peasant couldn't get out, that's what the by-passer saw. That's straight racist garbage? And this morning this same gutter press called our press release, which I have here and it is for you to judge whether the tone and the words were not justified, 'hysterical'. This is what one expects from the New Labour and the Tory papers such as the *Telegraph* whose reporter saw fit to comment on the clothes I was wearing and my body language. For God's sake, a guy has been kidnapped and they want to talk about whether my sari was above my ankles or what?

And here, for your entertainment, is an inside item in yesterday's *Mail On Sunday*. It says:

KIDNAP IN EDEN? SNAKE INTERCEDES.

Interseed and Intercede, get it?

I suppose they think that's funny. Oh, I can see one or two of you think it's funny too and I hope that you are laughing at them rather than with them.

As you know, the newspapers found Madhu before the police did. Which tells you something, doesn't it? He claims now, from the luxury of a suite at the Holiday Inn, that he went of his own free will and that he is a guest in this country and is free to go where he wants.

Of course their point is to attack us. There is an article by a so-called environmental scientist who says short stem grain, wheat and rice do no harm. That's it, do no harm. Nothing about the eco-balance, the devastation and non-renewal of top soil, the destruction of the countryside by weed-killer and poison-resistant crops ... just an attack on my work.

I am glad to have this opportunity to clear things. I am not, as one newspaper reported, out on bail. I have not been charged with any offence and I won't be. The police asked me stupid questions and let me go. Oh yes, they kept me and were sarcastic, but that's to be expected. Are the cops on the side of ordinary people or the multinationals? They warned me against going back to the Holiday Inn or trying to get in touch with Madhu again. Yeah, 'go figure' as the Americans say.

I had been, as I told them, to the Holiday Inn last night to speak to Madhu. It is not true that I broke the door down or that I smashed up the equipment in his room. It is an absolute, misogynist lie to suggest as they did in the interview this morning, and that's your so-called impartial, sit-on-the-fence BBC – and I have a few things to say about the dishonesty of the woman reporter on that occasion as well – that I assaulted the officials from Interseed. The official was of course a 'minder' who had been assigned to Madhu once he turned Judas.

I can tell you what I saw in the room though. Madhu was watching TV with his minder. I don't know what they were watching but the one glimpse I caught of the screen made me feel that it is what the *Sun* calls 'adult entertainment'.

He was very nervous confronting me and that's to be understood. I politely reminded him that he had this major session to address at the International Conference, that the press and TV would be there, that we had worked together for months and that in fact Eden's sponsors had paid for his ticket to England and for all his conference expenses. He had come here as a volunteer and I reminded him of the send-off that his village committee and other villagers from the territories affected by the GM crops that Interseed is experimenting with in their territory, had given him. They relied on him and trusted him to convey the message of their experience to the world – how the effects of the short stem, short-term gains had turned to disaster for the land and for their lives.

The Interseed employee minder tried to stop me speaking to him. Madhu didn't say a word all the time and then, at a nod from his minder, says very meekly, almost afraid to open his mouth, 'Virginia, I don't want to speak with you. I am here because I wanted to be. You must leave me alone.'

I couldn't believe my ears. He doesn't speak like that. He's been drugged or programmed. It was like talking to a cult member.

I tried to get through. I said, of course we aren't paying our speakers. The conference is a cooperative effort but the sponsors would be disappointed. I told him that it would have wide repercussions in India. He didn't know what to say to that.

Some of you have seen Madhu around the conference and at the Organic Fair. He had been on the Indian vegetable stall for the first two days of the week, and you know what a genial, outgoing, eager personality he is. He was transformed. It wasn't normal, so I put it to him straight, have they drugged him? The minder laughed, so I asked Madhu if he had slept.

I looked around the room. There were piles of presents that he had bought. There were bags from Oxford Street, and designer clothes for himself and probably for his teenage children strewn on the bed. And gadgets. The worst kind of consumerism you can think of. Electronic game machines, playstations or whatever it is they are called.

'So where's the flat-screen cinema-sized TV?' I asked and before his minder could intervene, Madhu said, 'Downstairs.'

'So you've bought this witness from the South?' I asked the Interseed man.

'We've paid Mr Devdar not one penny.'

'Of course not, but you've bought all this crap for him.'

'I am only telling the truth, Virginia,' Madhu says.

'Oh no, you're not. You are telling the newspapers a pack of lies about short stem crops and the fertilizer and built-in pesticides that are playing havoc with the ecocycle of Rajasthan. You are not telling them the same story you told us, Madhu.'

How to get to him? For a moment I thought he might come over and leave all that stuff on the bed and go down and out of the hotel and back to this conference. I invited him to. Another man came in and it was at this point that they started to physically assault me. They must have been afraid that Madhu would turn double Judas, or that he'd see sense and return to us. I said they should not touch me and that I refused to leave till I got an answer from Madhu.

I looked at Madhu's face. Like he'd been beaten. And you know what the wankers did? They shoved him in the bedroom and locked the door. Of course I battered on it and fought them off. They couldn't take that. They didn't expect a woman to fight back. I said I wasn't leaving until they released their prisoner.

They didn't touch me themselves. They sent for female security. You know why they have female security at that place? To throw prostitute women out after some guy has used them or when they haven't been given an adequate bribe to let them in to do their dangerous work.

I wasn't going to be manhandled by these women. They were doing their job. If the men wanted to throw me out, they would have to do it themselves and so I threw myself at them, defying them to do their own dirty work.

'You can't go back with all these bribes. Your people will know you are a traitor, a Judas, with your damned pieces of silver around you,' I shouted to Madhu through the door and tapped on it to get his attention above the shouting and misogynistic abuse these guys were laying on me.

I am not particularly proud of the incident and, friends, Eden 2000 has bigger things to do than to expose the petty tactics of Interseed. But think about how I feel. I have worked in Rajasthan for a year trying to get information about the potential destruction that GM crops and global greed can do to the sometimes illiterate victims. The Indian government are completely complicit in this rape of their land and their ecosystems and the suppression and exploitation of their people's lives.

So OK, suppose one concedes that he wasn't kidnapped, just lured away. What was the point of keeping his whereabouts secret for four days, even from the police? And what went on in those four days?

This buying spree of vulgar consumerism? Some brainwashing techniques? Rest and recreation? And I wonder what they

provided for him in that time – only *visual* adult entertainment?
You bet I'm bitter.

But let's not miss the opportunity that Madhu has given us
by his defection. We can face defectors. After all, the enemy
we are up against is the great servant of mammon in our time
and they are global, they are loaded and they are ruthless. This
story tells us just how ruthless.

So, you press people and the three cameras – You want a
story? It's not a kidnap or a hysterical woman breaking down
doors and smashing game stations and in the process attacking
gentlemanly bio-executives. It is a story of greed and bribery
of stopping at nothing. Of corrupting innocence just as they
have corrupted the lands on which the unsuspecting live. What
they've done to Madhu Devdar is your story. I defy you to give
him a blood test or a urine sample test. You'll find out. That's
your job. And if they didn't drug him, doesn't it show us that
they plumb new depths? Isn't this just the tip of the iceberg?
I challenge you to report it as it actually is. Not that there's
much hope of that with ninety per cent of media shares owned
by globalized interests.

Friends, thank you.

Main sirf Hindi mey bol sakti hoon, aap uska tarjomah kar
deejeyeh ... I can only speak in Hindi but you can translate
it as you wish. I am just a humble farmer's wife, and yes, you
can say you have given me something of a shock. When you
came and told me two days ago that he was missing in Britain

and asked if he had any enemies there, I wasn't sorry, I was actually glad that the bastard was undergoing some troubles there. No, I am not bitter about him at all. But what do you expect? Only he is quite happy now to abandon his wife and his children and roam around the world with other sorts of people. I am sorry, no offence meant to you.

What you say is quite right. This village has ceased to be an island. All sorts of people come through from the cities and God only knows where. They say America, London, Holland, including you with all this equipment. You can't walk anywhere in this village without tripping over a tractor or smelling this filthy oil they use in it.

When I was a girl, and that wasn't so long ago you know – how old do you think I am? – they traded me off to my children's father. I was an innocent and ignorant child, even before I started my womanly maturities. There was nothing here on the bones of my chest. His family wanted me for gathering sticks and milking cows and for the joy of their boy in future.

And hunger there was then. In the whole district. The crops would fail, the rains would fail, God was the God of failure. Then the same year the river would flood.

Even so in my time as a girl the government people came down and started digging some wells, so instead of walking ten miles, you had to walk three. In those days the grasshoppers, locusts and weevils would eat up half the grain and the rest would be eaten by rats after the harvest.

Then the government and white man opened the office in Dhanpur village and all the farmers were called. Nobody went except one fellow from Dhanpur, a low-caste fellow whose landlord had died leaving nobody, and the swine had squatted the land. He was afraid of nothing, because he was godless. The Dhanpur farm office was offering free seeds with magic in them. They would grow very short and even at that height yield a harvest and then they would grow again and give more seed. This bastard untouchable fellow started one year. Everyone in the village said he would be cursed by the gods for trying things that our grandfathers hadn't tried. We used manure for enriching the soil and the weevils and locusts we had to just beat off. The rats no one, not God nor man, can do anything about. The rains failed that year and still this fellow's crops came out and then came out again. It was unnatural. It was a sort of magic but the government scientists came by the busload to examine what he had done and he became rich overnight.

That was when people in our village thought they would speak to the Dhanpur project. My children's father went. It took us three years and then we were growing all sorts of short stem grain. My children's father bought a watch, new utensils for the home, beds for everyone, a tractor which we can use as a pump in our own well. The crop was not only doubling, it was keeping the insects away from nibbling it all to death. Everything that Dhanpur told us we were doing. My children's father had great faith in them, if they had sold him poison he would have drunk it.

Then *she* came to tell us it *was* poison. Telling us that our new gold was poison. Bhagwan! Who was this churail, this witch? Uninvited she came with her fellows. She was there in the fields every day and the farmers first laughed at her and then started listening because we are not rude people in this part of the country. She was our guest and we fed her and she started wearing our native clothes and threw off her jeans and shirts. She was saying if you kill the bugs, you kill the soil. That the roots of the new plants were too deep and soon all our water would be finished, that all the fertilizer powder that the Dhanpur men were selling was poison and our land would go back to being a desert soon.

Nobody listened to her. Nothing of what she said was happening, but she said it would happen in the next year and the year after next and in our children's time. Like some cheap astrologer. And then my children's father invited her to my house. It is his house and it is not my place to say anything. She was not clean. She said water is precious and would not bathe. And all the time she was preaching all this about the seed we used being bad and she began shamelessly speaking to the men about doing our *kaka* in the fields. And then some men made her shut up and told her that for thousands of years everyone goes to the fields anyway to relieve.

Well the truth is that our family and thousands of other families in this area had just got out of debt, because of all the gold seed and because of the Dhanpur magic.

My father and gradfather used to say our life is ruled by debt only. That's how I was born – in debt, got married in debt and would have died in debt. But now this kalyug, the blighted age seemed to be passing. We could at last pay. It was a miracle. It was true we owe the Interseed man each year but he didn't take too much. He wanted a percentage of what we sell which is less than what the landlord and moneylender would take from us. And this Virginia didn't stay long enough to make her witch's predictions come true.

But witch she was because I caught her in the fields on top of my husband with her skirt raised to her chest and his dhoti and underwear cast aside. They were sweating in joy and doing it, this bathless woman and my husband, my God how they were doing it! Yes. I stood there for minutes and they were doing this shamefully, with no care for the sights or sounds or for who was looking because their joy made them invisible. Or so they thought. But I saw them and my heart went into my stomach, like a fast-setting sun.

I waited for him to come back and for her to start pretending to help me with the cooking by peeling potatoes and then I turned and slapped her. Oh she knew what it was for. My fingers were marked on her cheek and she clutched it. It was a stinging slap and I said, 'Now leave my house, you defiler of lives.' My children's father was like a mouse.

I threw her out of the house. She was eating my food, sleeping under my roof and taking my husband's seed. Then she looked at him. I said, 'I saw you both, so my eyes have bled with the sight of you. Now go.'

He began to argue and said I had seen nothing, I must have eaten bhang leaves like my father and brother before me and had false visions.

'Son of a three-legged bitch, you can go too,' I said and spat in her face and in his.

They went, God help me. They went that day because they saw I was on fire and no words and lies could put me out. I said nothing that day or in that week to my children and I would forever have kept the reason for their father's going from them, but he shamelessly started touring the villages with Virginia and preaching all this rubbish about short stem crops destroying the world in ten years' time. Everyone felt sorry for me as I mastered the driving of the tractor and did the work in the field by myself now. And all the time as I drove the tractor, and saw the mud being dug and churned behind me, I wished it was the white woman's guts.

And then he went away from our part of the country and she went too. He sent a message ten days ago. The man from the Dhanpur project brought the letter which he sent by wire. He was begging my forgiveness. He said he got to England and found that this dirty woman had men whom she had slept with there. They were jealous of this brown, laughing fellow she had brought back – ignorant peasant chap. One of her men said he would fight him. My children's father complained to the bathless woman. Then the bathless tells him that she is a woman and she can go with whom she likes. He said that is not good and she told him that he had done what he liked when he climbed on her and kept me without knowledge of it. Women and men were the same. My Madhu didn't understand it. Women and men don't even look the same. So he asks if I will take him back. I told the Interseed man to use the wire and tell him 'yes'. Then he sends another wire to say what about the children, will they forgive him? And I send a wire back to say that he has to bring some presents, like good TV and the things you can see on the TV and clothes. They will see the presents that daddy brings from UK and they will be happy and forgive him. Then he sends a wire back saying he will have to die because he has no money and now his children will never forgive him. I got very worried when he said he had no money for presents for the children and was going to tell him never mind for the presents, just come back here and we will rejoice in your return and we will never talk about the bathless woman, but my wire was late and his wire through the computer machine in Dhanpur reached me first. Now he says he has money, that he is buying gifts and will be coming soon and then he himself told me, if I hear that someone has captured him, it is not true and that only the mother of his children has captured his heart forever.

SEVEN

jig jigolo

From: KKKNYLAW@aol.com

To: Khannatravels@yahoo.com

Dear Sirs,

We are a firm of New York solicitors and we are in search of a Mr Suresh Khanna of London whose postal address in that city was some years ago, on information received, 11 Stansgate Gardens, Notting Hill. If such a person is known to you, would he please get in touch with the above e-mail address as he may learn something to his advantage to do with the disposal of the estate of a Mrs D Zimmermann who was his neighbour at the time.

Peter King

(Of King, Karlin and Kornilovski, KKKNYLAW)

From: Khannatravels@yahoo.com
To: KKKNYLAW@aol.com

Dear Mr Kornilovski,

You're looking for Suresh Khanna? Ex of Stansgate Gardens,
Notting Hill. You've found him. I remember Dorothy Zimmermann
with great affection. She was my neighbour for several years and I
always looked after her. I was quite distraught when she left to see
her daughter and never came back. The landlord told me she had
given up her room and had informed him of the same by post. It
was, however, 10 Stansgate Gardens.

Nevertheless, I have always wanted to know what happened to my
dear friend and you have now established contact with me for which I
am grateful. I would of course wish to know immediately the content
of any communication you have for me. I can send you my snail-mail
address and the name of my solicitors is S. Battiwalla, 16 Rumpole
St London E1, if you need to be officially in touch with them.

Yours truly,

S. Khanna

From: Patsyl4481@ammetro.com
To: Khannatravels@yahoo.com

Hi Suresh,

I can't believe it's been twenty years. Check the date which goes
with my name on the address of the e-mail? Can I flatter myself
that you too remember it? It's dedicated to you and the twelve
glorious days we spent together in London and in England starting
that April.

Whew! Twenty years and you know how long it took me to track you down? I tried all the Khannas at Hotmail and Yahoo, starting with numbers. Hey, I have sent eight-hundred-odd e-mails looking for you and then I remembered your dream which you once let slip, between sleep and wake, so to speak, when you said you'd like to own a travel business with the cash you put by. I asked you why and you said, 'What else can a gypsy do?'

And that was somewhere in my head and I pulled it out and 'e'd a girl in London and she located the directory and found that you weren't at Gypsy travels. But I should have known you'd name your dream after yourself. So Khanna travels it is and I am lucky to have found you.

Just wanted to say hi, revive some memories.

With fond endurance, respect and wonder,
Patsy K

From: Khannatravels@yahoo.com

To: Patsy14481@ammetro.com

Dear Patsy,

Yes, I remember you. But what the hell are you doing tracking me down like this?

And what is this about Dorothy Zimmermann and her estate? Who is Kornilovski and why did they write to me and how do you come into it? Are you connected with the law firm? Is it a will in which she has left me something or what?

Please get back to me straight away.

Suresh

From: Patsy14481@ammetro.com
To: Khannatravels@yahoo.com

Dear Suresh,

Take it easy. I found you, so you can't run away. It's a business address, isn't it? And in answer to your questions – you could have asked how I've been, instead of rushing in with them, or what I'm doing – KKK is the firm my ex-husband founded with Karlin and King. The partners owe me and pay me and look after my estates. I used their e-mail because it's cheaper to do it from the office, that's all. In fact, I was sitting in my late husband's office. It was his wish that nothing should be disturbed and the office should be left as it was and the nameplate still pinned to the door. So even though Kornilovski has been dead for twenty-one years and seven months, his name is alive and his desk is active with papers and I use it and that's not so bizarre because when I walk through that door and sit at that desk and shuffle my share portfolios, my name is still Kornilovski, and will remain, even if I remarry, God bless him.

So that's how. But you? I suppose you're a prosperous businessman by now. So we can meet as equals perhaps. You always felt at such a disadvantage with your empty pocket and your bare room and your dashing looks and your one possession which was the black address book that went with the polished phone.

Oh don't I remember, the attic and the rain and your narrow bed and how I insisted on going there from the hotel and how reluctant you were – how you led me a dance all over London before we could finally go back to your 'hovel' as you called it. And for all that the three days there, cooking for you on the gas ring and shopping in Portobello market and drinking at your pubs, Finch's and Heneky's (you see I remember the names), were happy. You don't know how they helped me, or maybe you do ... but the memory revives gratitude and old desires like dull roots with spring rain ...

Please write less officiously, Suresh. Please?

Still Patsy14.4.81

From: Sureshk007@yahoo.com
To: Patsy14481@ammetro.com

Patsy,

Don't ever write that trash to me at the official address. Let me off that old hook and write at this address which is my private e-mail. All my employees and god knows who else can look into the other e-mails. I would have thought a mature woman like you would have more sense. Anyway, I don't want you to write anything to me at all.

Except you didn't answer my question. Who at your law firm is dealing with Dorothy Zimmerman's will? I want to know straight away what all this means and how much money there is.

Suresh

From: Patsy14481@ammetro.com

To: Sureshk007@yahoo.com

So it's 007 now is it? Isn't that a bit dated? Funny how, when I was looking for you, I didn't think of it. But I am sure you are as handsome, suave and dashing as ever and deserve the accolade of that overused number.

But my dear, please don't be annoyed. I remembered your kindness to old Mrs Zimmermann and her name stuck in my head because it's Bob Dylan's original name and I had a dream about how it would be strange if this were really Bob Dylan's long-lost mother marooned in Notting Hill through the Second World War which she always spoke about.

I remember the conversation so very clearly. She was ill and you heated her some soup and we took it down one floor to her room below together and you sat her up in bed and she ate it. I think it was called 'cock-a-leeky' and you got it from a can and I couldn't believe the name of the soup and you didn't realize that it could stand for something rather disgusting. And I sat on the bed and she knew I was American and talked of the yanks she had met during the War and how she was only a girl then and had joined a women's corps to make ammunition and she got you to rummage in her wardrobe and bring out a box with photographs of the girls standing next to a bomb they had made. I remember she told us about how she was the only Jewish girl and she felt she was completely accepted in the corps and in the factory where they did quality control of the bombs.

So it was that memory that prompted me to use her name when looking for you.

I want to be straight with you, Suresh, because I have this overwhelming feeling that we shall be friends again (and more?) and I must confess, I thought it likely that your old Mrs Zimmermann was dead. I knew you'd moved away because I've been to London

several times since '81 and I've always gone on a pilgrimage to
11 Stansgate Gardens and gazed up at the attic and talked to the
present occupants who have bought the building and live there,
occupying all five floors with their kids and their nanny and au pair.
And now I feel such a fool, because I've been going and gazing at
the wrong building all these years, the wrong house. Of course
it wasn't 11. It was 10, but they must have painted the doors and
the outside because it all looks and feels not like the slum it was.
But you were gone anyway.

I thought that using Mrs Zimmerman's name and the sniff about
the will, which of course there isn't, would get you to respond,
so forgive the little subterfuge. Remember what Portia says in
Merchant? To do a great right, do a little wrong.

Lots of love,

Patsy

From: Sureshk007@yahoo.com
To: Patsy14481@ammetro.com

No, I fucking don't remember what Portia says to anybody. I don't
read Shakespeare's novels, remember?

So that's the game, right? There isn't any Zimmermann and no will,
and no cash. You don't know what you've done. I am in a bad way.
The business is in a bad way. I've got a family to support in a style
to which they have become accustomed and you raised my hopes.
I should have known it was some con-artist. It was the best e-mail
I've had all month and now you tell me it was shit – dreamed up
by your sick, old mind. Well damn you, bitch. I was relying on the
money and began to think how much it was. Mrs Zimmermann was
my genuine friend. I may have been poor and a bum and sold myself

to bitches like you, but she didn't know any of that. She liked me and trusted me and you struck it lucky when you used her name because it's perfectly possible that if she had had any loot she'd have left me some if she thought about her last two years on earth.

Don't write to me again. I've got enough troubles.

From: Patsyl448l@ammetro.com
To: Sureshk007@yahoo.com

My dearest 007,

Has anyone told you how charismatic you look and sound when you fly off the handle? There's no need. OK, you need some money. I got money.

Does that ever come between friends?

And what do you mean she didn't know?

When you went out to have a leak, Mrs Zimmermann confided in me. Shall I tell you how it went?

'I can see you're Jewish.'

'No, but my late husband was. I am a WASP.'

She didn't get that.

'Look where I've landed up. There's a coloured girl, takes in and has Arabs downstairs and there's our coloured boy upstairs, your Suresh, God bless him. I've got nothing against the coloureds but they all seem to be in the business, you know, on the game.'

Then she grabbed my wrist. 'Forgive me, I thought I was talking to a Jewish girl, like me. You see you are not one of his clients. He couldn't bring his clients back here. The landlord told me that he is a fancy man; he goes to hotels to do their bidding.'

Oh yes, she knew and she was telling!

How we do deceive ourselves. But she said she genuinely loved you and said you helped her up the stairs when she broke her leg and had to stay sitting on the landing in agony till you came home early in the morning and how she never went out without assistance after that.

Well, Suresh, if you don't want me to write, I guess this is adios.

XXXX

Patsy

From: Sureshk007@yahoo.com

To: Patsy14481@ammetro.com

My Dear Patsy,

It's the stress – I suppose you understand. It wasn't really the money, I was just disappointed at not really having a way of knowing what happened to old Dorothy Zimmermann for whom I cared as though she was a grandmother. I was lonely in London in those days and she was someone to come home to, even though our building was always silent and dark, because the guys on the first floor didn't believe in capitalism or science and the modern world and never paid electricity bills and only used candles. The basement was full of the landlord's stolen goods, which he did as a sideline. The first floor was Marlene, the good-time Trinidadian, who was always out with Arabs till dawn and then slept the whole day, spent four to ten making herself up and was off out again at ten. And then Mrs Z with her reading lamp and me in the attic.

Yes, of course I remember that great little time we spent in the flat and then around England. I secretly think of it as my honeymoon.

It's nice to be tracked down by you, even though I remember that we had sealed our relationship with a kiss and promised never to try and get in touch again. But 'never' is not a word you can use in life. 'Never' never comes true. So here we are again. And I know and hope you know that it's different now. It's bound to be, we've moved on. But your suggestion is good, we could remain friends ...

X

Suresh

From: Patsyl4481@ammetro.com
To: Sureshk007@yahoo.com

Dear Suresh,

Friends? Friends? What's that? A TV sitcom? I want to meet you again. You say where. I'll send you a ticket – hah, is that a joke??? – you deal in tickets, don't you? You could hop over to NY right now or send me a ticket or I'll get one and come over. Same time, same place. The Dorchester? Or has it deteriorated? Shall we go somewhere else? How about the little hotel you took me to in Wales? Can we go back there?

Just grab a few days for a start? I'm busy too.

Suresh, I'll put my cards on the table, sweetheart. I have thought about you as a thirsty traveller thinks of the oasis, an image in the distance, unattainable, desirable, the only salve for a fever so deep that it racks my skeleton.

Ever since K died – and that's when you picked me up, derelict and lonely in London, surrounded by all the trappings of wealth, but as you said then 'poor in spirit, because everything had been taken away when he was snatched from me' – I had lost all idea of what life was about. All dressed up and nowhere to go. Like an old woman stumbling into rooms not remembering what she came for. Except the thirst. The thirst for love. And I didn't hide it, honey. I faced up.

You were the shrink and the masseuse and the cowboy who rode into town at a minute past high noon, all combined in one. You were more – you were Sir Gallahad. I bless the phone call I made from that little directory in the hotel room which one of the staff brought me. He said I wouldn't regret it. He didn't smirk, which was the first reassuring sign. I had been to restaurants, a limo tour of London. I was still alone ... I never told you any of this. I remember telling you a friend passed on the agency's phone number – and fighting myself not to open that book and call 'Dicky Bowe Male Escort Agency'.

And the rest is history. You were kind and polite. I didn't realize till afterwards at dinner when you confessed that you didn't know who Mozart was and had never been to an orchestral concert. I remember thinking how sharp you must have been to pick up the fact that you were not to applaud between movements. And you said you were watching everyone else and doing in Rome as the Romans did.

That was handsome of you. And handsome? I couldn't keep my hands off you, but didn't know how to ask, because I had never had an 'escort' before and suddenly it seemed OK and not needy and desperate and American because you made it so easy. Such a gentleman, no awkwardness, no stain of commerce in our smooth and beautiful transition to intimacy.

Oh yes, I told myself that you were the professional, that's all, but my heart kept pounding and hoping that it was more than that; that your gentleness was the result of real emotion. That's all I could hope for – some human response that wasn't pity for the American who may not have been young and taut and fresh as spring but didn't deserve to feel old.

And I remember the kindness and the romance. I don't know how we did it, but those twelve days are the most memorable of my life. Suresh, I have had men before and after. This was a tragic period of my existence, as I told you, I loved old Korni, though he was pretty much an autocrat and wanted to keep a woman in her place. And his death devastated me and I took the trip to England after more than a year, determined to play the widow, but attracted and convinced finally to play the field.

We never discussed it, afraid I suppose that it would interrupt the champagne haze, the drives of strikingly cold and fresh air, the little spliffs of marijuana which you so lovingly rolled for me, the shopping sprees in Oxford and Bond street when I bought you shirts and suits and myself some diamonds – but didn't you feel that I too wasn't giving everything I should give as a woman when we were intimate? If you did, yes, it was true. I was still pining, still looking back, still unable to engage you fully as a woman, as a body, as a partner in the ecstasy granted to us. (Hey, I don't mean that religiously, I know how much you hate religious nonsense – what did you call it? 'The American vulnerability.' I loved, and recall so often, your parody of Americans prostrate before lying, cheating and stupid-faced Indian gurus, fools falling for confidence tricksters. I've tried to repeat it for friends from Maine to Mexico, and they get it and they laugh and it's still true, but only you do it so good! So true!)

We can discuss all this now coolly, can't we? But maybe I am going on too long, Maybe to you I was just a fortnight's fun. Oh well.

Still XXXX
Patsy

From: Sureshk007@yahoo.com
To: Patsy14481@ammetro.com

Patsy My Dearest,

What do you mean a fortnight's fun? You turned my world upside down. I have thought of it since and constantly. Like you, I came upon our mutual experience unexpectedly. I was young and Indian and desperately struggling in London to be recognized. I wanted to be a model as I told you, but the agencies wouldn't take brown faces. I was pissed off with London and offered myself to this escort agency, Dicky Bowe and they took me on. Only later on, I found out that they'd put me on what the girls in the office called the 'kinky register' for clients who wanted black and maybe even Asian escorts.

But finding you was different. How could I lie? It was my job, but in the first few minutes of knowing you, the job was gone. I told you. It was as though I was going through the process of picking up a girl I'd seen and fancied, a girl in a club, a girl in the select set, the prettiest girl at the party, a stranger across a crowded room. And yes, you responded. Remember the dance after the concert on the little dance floor of the restaurant. My hand shivered as I held you, wondering whether to pull you closer or whether you'd think it was brazen and cheeky and going too far. How far could I go?

But you understood my hesitation. It was so comfortable to have your experience behind the frantic and clumsy contact we were trying to turn into an elegant romance ...

But how can I put all this in an e-mail? I nearly said 'on paper' but time has moved on and here we are communicating through the ether, between the stars.
Please reply.

Of course kisses XX
Suresh

S Battiwalla

16 Rumpole St

E.1

Dear Suresh,

You don't reply to my e-mails, so I have to send a hand-delivered letter. As your solicitor I have to warn you that the creditors, especially the VAT office and Messrs J. Bratby and sons are threatening immediate action in the courts and they have briefed Counsel. We don't have the finances to fight the claims. You don't seem to realize the seriousness of the matters in hand. I am trying to get your personal property exempt from liabilities, but PLEASE TALK TO ME.

Savak

From: Khannatravels@yahoo.com

To: Battiwalla@BTnet.co.uk

Dear Savak,

I am off to New York tomorrow. This is it! I hope to bring back a sufficient loan, or even some earnings which will not be repayable, at least enough to hold off the VAT man and the bastard Bratby, whom I should counter-sue because the building he sold us has had to have endless repairs. Anyway, the deal won't concern you, it will be a personal loan with no security.

I promise all bills will be paid by the end of the week on my return. I may take a few days holiday in the States but between you and me, that will also be business, so don't go blow your stupid trumpet to Nita.

Yours confidently,

Suresh

From: Patsy14481@ammetro.com

To: Sureshk007@yahoo.com

Dearest Suresh

That was a lovely, lovely letter.

Thank you.

All these years, yes I've had lovers, but I remember the young man, the lithe brown body who gave generously of himself and was hungry for my love, who drank of me like a street urchin begging for pennies and with an open begging palm. And then when I let them drop, tossed them up to play heads and tails and clapped them in his hands to determine my fate.

Suresh, let's meet, let's relive those times.

I am not naive. I know that I am twenty years older, but I have had some assistance from science and medicine and you will be surprised, I think. And below the waist, all is the same, nothing withers.

And you? I remember the care, the caution you always had in your gentle yet fiery eyes. I asked you what you did for a living. Of course it was a pretence, a game and you said you were by profession a consultant on love. Then so many days later you told me that the Indian jokey word for getting it on was 'jig-jig' and I never told you this, but in my mind you were always my 'jig-jigolo'. It made it so much more acceptable to me, until of course the thought went away. I came looking for services and went away finding love. And still it lingers.

Why do I think of you with a hundred million males of eligible age in America? Because there was something pure in your giving and, above all, because you are the only man who has ever understood me. I regret having made the vow, the promise to never get in touch. I should have carried you away from London and brought you with me to New York and kept you in a closet and taken you out each night to dine and dance and make love ... You were so handsome, so beautiful, a tiger, a warm wind with the fragrance of trees, a distant mountain, a frothy gurgling stream, a pin-up and a whole maze, a labyrinth of personality behind those eyes ...

See? I can still describe you. Where, when, how?

All my love
Patsy

_____

From: Sureshk007@yahoo.com
To: Patsy14481@ammetro.com

Dearest Patsy,

You'll have to change that from Patsy14481 to 21701, because I'm on my way to New York. I hate to ask you this, but I've left my cards in the country, and impatient as I am to meet you, am flying out today, so can you book me a room with your credit cards at a hotel of your choice where we are destined to start again? I'd hate to book into a hatel you hote, or hotel you hate, and New Yorkers are so particular about the particular virtues of hotels, I'm wary of offending.

Yes? XX
Suresh

From: Patsy14481@ammetro.com
To: Sureshk007@yahoo.com

Dearest S,

It's the Cameron on 2nd Avenue 68th Street. What's your flight? I've got a face job at 3.40, which I don't feel like cancelling because I want you to have me at my best and she's the greatest in Manhattan and that's got to be in the world and booked every minute so I can't cancel and rebook, but you understand the room is in your name but I've got to give them an impression of my card, so wait in the lobby.

Whoopee! Do we know what we're getting into? You've studiously told me nothing about yourself, but suppose I told you that I've been doing a bit of nosing around and know that you are married, live in Harrow and have two teenage daughters and that they are twins and eighteen? So marriage and babies three years after me, eh? Blown away or what?

Don't be, I know more.

XXXX
Your
Patsy

From: Sureshk007@yahoo.com
To: Patsy14481@ammetro.com

Where the hell are you? I waited eight hours in the lounge of the Cameron. I have searched the other hotels in the area, thinking maybe you made a mistake and have come back. Sunday and everything's shut. I went downtown to the offices of your KKK law firm and the black security geezers threw me out and nearly broke my shoulder. They wouldn't let me in the building and they said they didn't have an emergency number for your firm, which is a lie. They won't let me have a room till they see your credit card.

Please, please get here. I don't have cards myself as I told you and I am not carrying much cash – just enough for a coach back to the airport. I was relying on our whirlwind romance for food, clothes and shelter. You asked this waif and stray to cross the pond and Patsy I'M HERE! I'm e-mailing this from the Commerce Club of the hotel – they felt sorry for me when I explained and allowed me to use the free facility. I had to give them your name. The clerk had heard of your late husband's firm – said they were big on suing hotels.

Waiting,
Suresh

From: Sureshk007@yahoo.com
To: Patsy14481@ammetro.com

Patsy darling,

I can't believe this. I hope nothing's happened to you. I stayed the night sitting in the lobby and then when they threw me out, walking the streets waiting for your office to open. You realize I don't have a phone number for you and that bitch receptionist at the office has been obviously instructed to not know who I am. She called the other black guys, the day shift, and they bodily threw me out. What are you playing at? Why did you call me here?

Reply at least. You can even now make it all right, even if you've had cold feet. Think of the time we spent in Edinburgh, walking in the castle and then in the car in the mountains in the Crofter's Retreat? I was hoping we could leave New York and you could show me some of these wide-open God's Acres.

I'll pick up my e-mail in half an hour again. You must get this. It's morning.

Suresh

From: Patsy14481@ammetro.com
To: Sureshk007@yahoo.com

Suresh,

Go back home. I'm sorry. Go back to Nita and your twins and your boy. See? I know. But that's not why you haven't seen me.

In fact you did see me. You looked right through me. I was wearing an orange skirt and jacket and shades and my hair's blonde again and the wrinkles don't show with the lights low.

But what's more I saw you. I came back into the Cameron lobby a second time to have a good look and make sure. And yes it was you.

My God, what did I expect? That you'd still be twenty-eight years old and supple as a God? No. Sure, I am not an idiot and I can figure that twenty years have passed for you as well as for me.

Suresh, have you read a book called *Love in the Time of Cholera* by

Gabriel Garcia Marquez? No, of course you haven't. Did I ever fall for your mind? Or is that like asking if one can trip over the breeze? Go and get it if you have any spare change and read it while you're waiting, or on the plane back. It's about love lasting through time and it's a lie.

I came to my senses when I saw the middle-aged man, going on fifty now, round with prosperity, with a pot belly over the belt, bald, bespectacled, eating a hamburger with ketchup staining the side of his mouth, not caring whom he was offending in the lobby. With a red plastic case with blue darts in it? Suresh, that was not the vision I carried about with me these last twenty years.

You've broken my heart looking for the boy who broke my heart and finding reality instead.

Go home. Good luck with the rest of your life. I'll piece mine together, never worry about old Patsy.

From: Sureshk007@yahoo.com

To: Patsy14481@ammetro.com

I was looking out for a seventy-five-year old too. You said you were fifty back in '81 but I wasn't born 13.4, baby, so I know you were giving yourself a five-year handicap at least. And maybe your teeth haven't fallen out because Americans get new ones and never mind the pain, don't they? What you're saying is the most immature stuff I've heard. You said let's be friends. Remember you called me. I didn't call you.

Of course I remember our whirlwind affair with great tenderness and if you give it a chance maybe you'll forget my partially bald head and the fact that I've put on a little bulk. Don't you notice, Patsy, how physical features fall away when you get into the spirit of another being?

I'll wait till this afternoon. Outside the hotel in the cold. I expect you to whisk me away in a limousine, my fairy princess.

Yours ever in anticipation, the same old,
Suresh

From: Patsyl4481@ammetro.com
To: Sureshk007@yahoo.com

It's no good. I know why you came. You want to get me to stake out a few thousand dollars for your failing business. I might have done, but why do we lie to each other? Has the whole fantasy been a lie? I may have money but I'm not playing that game again. I suppose I won't give it to you. I was prepared to see how we'd get on, to take you around the eateries of the Big Bagel, to hoist up the flag of your personality and see who saluted.

Yes, I've fooled myself. But not to that extent. I always suspected when you said you loved me that there was a false note in the harmony of the rich and heart-quickening chord.

And suddenly I'm free of you. You were the first guy since K died and I invested so much in that. I was looking at my own grief and my own deep, deep need and not at you who were, OK, generously, satisfying it. You dominated me and showed me the places you've probably shown other women you were hosting, but I never asked. It was new for me and I played the game of pretending it was new for you.

What are your kids called? Do they go to school? Maybe I shouldn't ask because that presumes we are friends and I guess you won't want to be.

Yours truly,
Patsy

From: Sureshk007@yahoo.com
To: Sbattiwalla@Btnet.co.uk

Dear Savak,

On plane back from States. Didn't work out. No cash. I guess it means close down and declare. It's the bastard Americans who have ruined the business. And Virgin. United and Branson have got their licenses to fly into Delhi, followed by a heap of other operators. The Indian government has thrown it wide open to these sharks and now the aircrafts are no longer crammed. The competition has cut the price of tickets to and from India and I can't sell, not at the margins I used to and not at all some weeks. So we small agents are fucked. What do I do, sell tickets to Kazakhstan? It's enough to turn one communist. I don't know what to do? We'll have to sell the house. Can you make an asset inventory please?

Suresh

From: Sureshk007@yahoo.com
To: Patsy14481@ammetro.com

Hello gorgeous,

This from the fat, bald, ageing man.

As the American said today, 'You want any kind burger, you want hippo burger, crocodile burger, elephant burger, you got it!'

You want the truth, you got it. Never mind your fancy books and Love with Cholera or Romance With TB or whatever.

In the Dorchester, in Grantchester, in the Wye valley, in Edinburgh, I was doing a job. I was a Gigolo or a Jig-Jigolo. That was my profession. I used to make old American ladies like you feel good and that meant fucking them when I didn't want to. That first time with you I went into the toilet of your hotel room and threw up. And it wasn't the Japanese food. It was your stink. Your sex smells, but it was my job. The way to your tight wallet was through your other loose bits.

And now lady lay, you are seventy-five. One foot slipping into that wooden box. The machine doesn't go on forever you know. You could have had a week of me and I'd have remembered my professional tricks and played them all for you.

Yes, of course I came for money. Why else? But when was it different? You conveniently forget. You had to beg me to say 'I love you'. You paid me in an increasing pile of fifty-pound notes. 'Stop saying it, Suresh, you have to *mean* it. I know I am paying you to say it but I'll pay you more to mean it.'

I've never forgotten that. I just thought to myself that these Americans are crazy. Paying me just to say it, yes, but paying me to mean it, knowing that I am just pretending a little deeper? You were so desperate and I put on such a good act. And when I took you to my room, reluctantly, to show you my poverty, it was part of the act of being in love. I wasn't reluctant at all. I was hoping you'd suggest buying me some furniture and you did.

In those days I carried some porn-pics in my wallet and quickly stimulated myself and swallowed my pride. Or the truth is I was an animal and would screw anything, even if with you I had to hold my nose half the time.

I may not have been able to manage the whole deal this time. You've got to be a pervert to have sex with an eighty-year-old dame.

My body is relieved that you let me down and I don't have to go

through that again. The reason I came is because I am desperate and I thought I'd go back to prostitution. Then I'd have to get the cash out of you with lies and then I'd have to find a way of leaving you and taking the cash back to England.
Keep it, Mrs Kornilovski.

Adios and no hard feelings. The truth prevails.
Suresh

From: KKNYLAW@aol.com
To: Khannatravels@yahoo.com

Dear Mr Suresh Khanna,

We are writing to you in the matter of the disposal of the estate of the late Mrs Patsy Kornilovski. If you have an attorney at law can you please forward us the name and address of the firm as we have to attend to this matter forthwith. All disclosures of bequest are made in the strictest confidence.

Yours truly,
Peter King
(Senior Partner, King and Karlin)

From: Sbattiwalla@Btnet.co.uk
To: KKNYLAW@ aol.com

Dear Peter King,

I act for the receiver in the estate of Mr Suresh Khanna who has these last few months voluntarily disappeared without trace after having declared bankruptcy. I have power of attorney and you may wish to advise me of any assets that are payable to Mr Khanna as the result of a bequest from the late Mrs Patsy Kornilovski. I am even now attempting to trace the whereabouts of Mr Khanna as are his family and Scotland Yard.

Yours Ever,
S. Battiwalla